WITH MASTERFUL PERSUASION HIS HANDS CARESSED HER. . . .

Hers mirrored the motion, reveling in his muscled torso as she touched his shoulders, his back, and the lean lines of his hips. Then she gasped and drew away, startled.

"Jed?"

"Shh, angel. It's all right. I won't hurt you," he crooned, his eyes deep and compelling, his hands bringing her back against his firm body. Even as the warning sounded in the recesses of her consciousness, she savored the haven of his steel-banded arms. For enigmatic as it seemed, he offered the intangible something she had craved. For whatever the nature of the power he held over her, she needed him. She did!

THE
ARDENT
PROTECTOR

Bonnie Drake

A CANDLELIGHT ECSTASY ROMANCE™

Published by
Dell Publishing Co., Inc.
1 Dag Hammarskjold Plaza
New York, New York 10017

Dell ® TM 681510, Dell Publishing Co., Inc.

Candlelight Ecstasy Romance™ is a trademark of
Dell Publishing Co., Inc., New York, New York.

ISBN: 0-440-10273-1

Printed in the United States of America
First printing—March 1982

Dear Reader:

In response to your continued enthusiasm for Candlelight Ecstasy Romances™, we are increasing the number of new titles from four to six per month.

We are delighted to present sensuous novels set in America, depicting modern American men and women as they confront the provocative problems of modern relationships.

Throughout the history of the Candlelight line, Dell has tried to maintain a high standard of excellence to give you the finest in reading enjoyment. That is and will remain our most ardent ambition.

Anne Gisonny
Editor
Candlelight Romances

To JED,
my third born

THE
ARDENT
PROTECTOR

CHAPTER 1

There had been no warning. The day was beautiful—as peaceful and clear a mid-May morning as any pilot could hope to encounter. The vista, as Montreal fell behind and the small Piper Arrow picked up its southeasterly flight path over the mountains of Vermont, was breathtaking, its sun-streaked palette an undulating ribbon of greens, flowing through the charcoals and hunters of pines and firs into the limes and yellows of newly budded spring growth.

They were headed home. The week had held a blend of culture and relaxation as Gillian had joined her parents for a long-overdue reunion. For Thomas and Sarah Montgomery, it was sheer pleasure to be with their daughter, who, too often in the past few years, had been a voice on the telephone rather than the physical presence they would have preferred. For Gillian, these days had recreated the warmth of her childhood, mercifully free, however, of the overprotectiveness that had finally driven her from her parents' home six years ago. It would have been all too simple, given her aversion to that stifling parental devotion, to burrow in her separate world, where she'd successfully established herself as a viable personality, a recognized and respected member of the art community. Yet, living the semisolitary existence that she did on an everyday basis, she had come to more deeply appreciate the backdrop of strength that her upbringing had allowed her. And having reached a point of basic self-assurance, she could genuinely enjoy her parents once again.

"Oh, damn!" Her father's grave tone, more than the oath itself, made her blood run cold. Only once before in recent memory had his voice carried that somber thread of desperation, but that had been in other circumstances beyond her understanding. Now, as she angled forward from her position diagonally behind him in the compact four-seater, her pale blue eyes flew in alarm to his fingers, suddenly tensed on the yoke, his own gaze fixed in dismay on the control panel of the small plane.

"Thomas?" Close by his right, her mother had caught it too, her face reflecting the same trepidation as did Gillian's.

Silently cocking his head toward the green gauge whose needle hovered around an ominous zero, he simultaneously depressed the yoke's mike button and began to speak into his headset, his first three words proclaiming the gravity of the situation.

"Mayday! Mayday! Mayday! This is two-nine-seven-two-Bravo. I'm at five thousand feet and losing oil . . ." The rest of his message was lost on Gillian, whose widened eyes met those of her mother, one slender hand reaching forward to grasp the arm of the older woman, while the other clutched frantically at the edge of the crushed velour seat. Even as a layman, she understood the problem. It was the oil that kept the engine moving smoothly; without it, there would quickly be overheating, then inevitable engine failure. In a momentary wave of panic, she became acutely aware of the smallness of the cabin, not much bigger than her own Volkswagen Rabbit and infinitely more vulnerable.

Yet Tom Montgomery was the best of pilots, an experienced flyer on this executive aircraft; surely he would handle the situation with his customary competence. Such spoke the hand that, in turn, covered hers reassuringly in lieu of words.

Calm, as Gillian had expected him to be, her father raised his voice just enough to be heard above the still steady drone of the engine, his words, now with a gentle touch, directed at his two passengers.

"The oil pressure is dropping. We'll have to go in." His

12

dark eyes pierced the tinted windshield as he began a desperate search through the growth far below, looking, looking for some possible place to put down his plane. It was tricky in the best of conditions, this mountain flying; given the present emergency and the presence on the airplane of the two people in the world nearest and dearest to him, the pressure on the pilot was awesome. His brief glance toward the wing disquieted him further, its gleaming metallic surface now streaked with oil strewn by the wind in a dark omen.

"We won't have more than another ten minutes before the engine quits on us. I'd like to get it down before that . . ." Ever the optimist, he remained true to form, his outward manner reflecting the same understated confidence that had made him a successful businessman.

Swallowing the knot of tension that had formed in her throat, Gillian forced herself to speak for the first time since the crisis had begun, trying desperately to control her rising pitch. "What's caused it, Dad? Is there nothing you can do?"

Her father's eyes never broke from their intent scrutiny of the landscape below, as he offered a ghost of a headshake. "No, sweetheart. Who knows? It may be a gasket that has split. Everything was checked out before we took off, but some things can go at any time, I'm afraid." His full attention returned to the ground below. "Now, if I can find a field or a riverbed . . ."

Gillian had always been totally complacent about flying; with her father in the cockpit, she'd never for a moment envisioned anything but a safe flight. Suddenly, with this agonizing turn of events, she was engulfed by a kind of fear that had nothing to do with her father's ability and everything to do with the simple facts of a small, fully fueled and cargoed plane, rugged terrain dominated by hills and mountains, and the unknown source of the problem and extent and consequences of the damage.

As the precious seconds ticked away and her father's search for an impromptu landing strip was interrupted only by his update of their position over the emergency frequency, Gillian was aware of a swell of helplessness washing over her as she sat, pulse racing, then faltering, then spurting ahead again.

"Okay, tighten your seat belts," her father began in a tautly controlled voice. "Sarah"—he glanced sideways, briefly, at his wife—"tighten that shoulder harness and unlock the doors." Pausing, he studied a narrow patch of brown earth far ahead and below them, before continuing as though reading from a manual. "Now, stay calm and listen carefully. I'm going to put down in that field. It's not terribly long and is surrounded by trees, but it's the only open area in sight." A final time he scanned the horizon, quickly reconfirming his claim. "I've slowed the plane down to ninety knots, and we're on a good glide path. I want you to put your heads in your laps. When we hit, stay down. When we come to a stop, I want you to get out as fast as you can. Do you understand?" His knuckles were white on the yoke, his eyes glued to the fast-approaching land.

Trembling from head to toe, Gillian did as he'd instructed, satisfied that her mother had done the same when the latter's hands reached to release both latches on the door by her seat, the craft's only exit. Showing his first real sign of unsureness, her father repeated his orders, raising his voice with a more personal urgency.

"Sarah, you open that door as soon as we stop and get out. *Get out!* Both of you! Get as far away from this plane as you can as quickly as you can. I will follow you, but I want you to move fast. We're carrying a full load of fuel . . ." His voice trailed off, the implication of his words obvious to both his wife and his daughter. An explosion would be fatal, even if they did manage to land intact.

Later Gillian was to recall the last moments of the

14

nightmare as a mélange of sensation—of heat and cold, of air pressure falling, of fear and relief, then absolute horror. Where there had been the static of the radio and the loud hum of the engine, there was suddenly a chilling silence as all mechanical functioning ceased. The buoyancy of flight gave way to a bone-shattering jolting, as the small plane touched, then bounced along the ground, tail down, moving at precarious speed along the furrowed earth.

So intent was she on surviving the jostling of her own slim body against the sides of the tiny cabin that she was unaware of the struggles of her father, sensing a too-rapid approach to the field's end, applying the brakes with every ounce of his strength only to find it inadequate, pulling up his flaps to slow the plane down, again falling short.

"We're going for the trees." She barely recognized the jarred timbre of the voice she'd known so well; it was, indeed, his moment of truth. "If I can squeeze between two of them, the fuselage and landing gear will slow us enough."

There was a tremendous clamor as luggage became dislodged and joined the frantic bouncing. A sharp pain seared Gillian's left arm, adding to the general shock of terror that enveloped her. She was to remember a deafening roar as the wings hit the trees and were brutally sheared off and then an impact of unbelievable force as the plane finally came to rest, beyond the trees, against the base of the foothills that Tom Montgomery had tried so desperately to avoid.

There were fragments of words she would recall in her struggle to escape the craft. Her father's voice . . . a command . . . sounds of unfathomable pleading . . . a heartrending scream . . . then, the explosion. All else faded into oblivion.

Slowly, very slowly, Gillian awoke. The sensations were there, yet they were totally different. All was quiet, inter-

15

rupted only by intermittent voices, soft and calm and seemingly directed at her, though she could not respond. There were tactile sensations, as her body made repeated contact with things human and those inert. Even the smells were new, overwhelmingly constant and undefinable. There was confusion, fear, pain, anguish—all touching her briefly between ripples of euphoric dissociation.

Only one presence could she identify—a recurring one that had neither name nor face yet possessed a vague place in her memory. Straining to see it, to hold it, to touch it, she failed. Yet it returned, faithfully, a single and mysterious link to her past in this strange and new setting.

"Good morning, Gillian," a singsong chime rang out, accompanied by the roll of a rising shade and then the bright burst of sunlight as Gillian timidly opened her eyes to confront the new day. "It's a magnificent morning once again—nice and sunny and warm. Not hot, mind you. But warm. We had just about enough of that terrible heat last week, now didn't we! Ach, what can we expect from the month of July, though, love—at least the air conditioning is working again. Wasn't that awful? I must say you were a good sport through it all. Well, I think I'll open the windows and let in some of the nice fresh air, for a change, before it heats up again!" The voice babbled on, its source busily moving around the room, talking out her every action even as her broad white-clad back remained to her patient. To Gillian's astonishment, the woman—or nurse, as her uniform implied—appeared to expect no response, as she turned on the faucet of the small sink and filled a basin with water.

"We'll get you all cleaned up this morning, as usual, and then you can listen to your radio again. Here, let me see about one of the new nighties Mr. Dawson brought you. What a lovely man he is—so thoughtful and considerate. And so good-looking . . ." The last was said more to herself than to her listener, though, indeed, so much of

16

the conversation had had that same ring. Even through her lingering grogginess, Gillian was bewildered. That she was in a hospital, that this was a nurse, she understood. There was that clean, antiseptic smell of her whitewashed environs that she recognized from earlier dreams. But how long had she been here? Who was this Mr. Dawson? She had *never* been a radio devotee! And why did this woman chatter on as though alone in the room?

"Ah, a lovely blue one," came the voice from the dresser by the windows. "Such a clever man, to pick a shade to match your pretty eyes so well!" With that note of admiration, she withdrew a neatly folded bundle before turning, with the nightgown in one hand and the filled basin in the other, finally, toward the bed. Gillian's baffled gaze, so unobservedly following the woman's every move, was suddenly met and held.

"Lordy! What a day! You're awake!" It was more of a shriek than an exclamation and was echoed by a look of such surprise on the kindly face that Gillian's confusion was confounded. "You're awake! You're awake!" Scurrying white feet brought the woman to the bedside in an instant, and though much of the wash water was lost in transit, it seemed irrelevant.

Despite her own perplexity, Gillian could not help but offer a shaky grin to the middle-aged woman whose round face, rosy cheeks, and twinkling eyes instantly reached out to befriend her. It was only when the nurse had repeated herself once more with a squealed, "You're awake!" that Gillian answered, weakly and in a near whisper, the fragment of a smile glinting off the corners of her lips.

"Of course I'm awake. The sun would have woken me, even if you had not!" She had always been an early riser, executing some of her finest pieces during the postdawn hours. It was in the morning that she had unbridled energy. That was, until now. She was unprepared for the enormous amount of effort that the small bit of speech had required. Lapsing into an exhausted silence, she ignored the many questions that had plagued her mind moments before, concentrating only on recapturing her strength to speak again. Mercifully, she needn't have worried about conversation, that being one of the outstanding qualities that had led to this particular nurse's special assignment to her case.

"Thank the Lord! You're awake! And how are you feeling, might I ask? A bit weak? Yes, well, that's only to be expected. But you're awake! Are you hungry?" With unbounded enthusiasm, the woman quickly deposited the basin and nightgown on the bedstand, all the while asking and answering her own questions. Strangely lethargic, Gillian was not sorry for her own purely incidental role in this interchange. "But of course you're hungry. And you'll have a *good* breakfast this morning. Thank the Lord! Oh, but I've got to get the doctor. He'll want to know about your progress. He'll be so pleased!" Gurgling exuberantly, she placed a pudgy hand on the limp one, as white as the soft blanket on which it lay. "Don't you move, love. I'm going to get the doctor. You'll be all right, won't you?" It took but a hair of a nod, superfluous at that, to release the woman. "Good! I'll be back in a jiffy."

With that, she whirled on a squeaky heel and made for the door, leaving in her wake a myriad of unanswered questions. Alone, Gillian faced her puzzling situation. How had she gotten here? Concentrating all her energy, she forced herself to return to the last conscious moment she had known. The plane—the plane and her parents . . .

"Gillian?" Either he'd been waiting just outside the door or her awakening had excited him as much as it had the woman who now followed excitedly on his heels. For whichever reason, Gillian's increasingly tormented train of thought was abruptly sidetracked by the appearance at her side of the doctor, white-jacketed and neat, pockets brimming with the few chosen tools of his profession. Her muddled consciousness took in a sandy-haired man, perhaps in his mid-thirties, whose medium height and build exuded comfort, whose serious expression barely camouflaged the eagerness in his eyes. "I'm Dr. Worthin. Welcome back!"

A faint smile was the only response she could muster, as Gillian dwelt on his very words. *Welcome back?*

"How do you feel?" His hand was cool on her wrist, in true doctorly fashion measuring her pulse.

Slowly and quietly, she made the effort of response. "Strange . . . weak . . . groggy." Her voice emphasized the same.

The eyes that studied her were reassuring, as was the grin that lightened his visage in relief at hearing her voice, faint though lucid. "It's no wonder! You've been through quite a bit. Do you know where you are?"

Evading the direction of the doctor's inquiry, Gillian could not ignore the thread of thought her memory had dredged up moments before. "My parents . . ." she rasped, "did they . . . are they here?"

The ensuing silence answered her question as powerfully as the pained look that the man tried unsuccessfully to hide. He'd been, frankly, unprepared for her alertness, after so long, let alone her awakening.

Gillian was numbed, refusing to accept what had so wordlessly been conveyed. "But we landed safely . . . we landed . . . I thought . . ." Her whispered pleading trailed off, her strength spent.

Peter Worthin's hand touched her shoulder in a gesture of understanding. "Everything possible was done, Gillian. It's a miracle that you're back with us. You've got a lot to catch up on." He had subtly shifted the focus of the discussion from tragedy to thanksgiving, succeeding inasmuch as she was suddenly incapable of concentrating on more than one issue at a time, and he had diverted her to another, skirting the blow that would hit her full force soon enough.

"Back?" A tremulous whisper escaped her lips.

Easing himself down onto the edge of the bed, he took her slim hand in his more solid one. How many times he'd done just this, he mused, when he'd doubted ever getting a response. As much as he would have liked to credit his medical attentions with her recovery, he knew instinctively that the matter had been out of his hands for weeks now. Medical science had indeed healed and preserved her body, yet it had been a partnership of her will and some higher force that had brought her back. "You've been in a coma. Do you remember anything of your time here?"

Time here? She remembered nothing of spending time here—or anywhere, for that matter. There had been a series of strange and disjointed dreams coming between the accident and her awakening today. Nothing else! Desolately, she shook her head.

"It's been seven weeks. You've been unconscious for seven weeks. No recollections?"

Seven weeks? How could that be? There was so little in her memory. Just fragments. There were voices, feelings, smells. All vague. All strange. All new. Except . . . except one. An odd familiarity of scent, the feel of a hand on her cheek, the croon of a voice by her ear. An odd but definite familiarity. But a disembodied wisp, floating aimlessly, like the others. The only thing she could remember that was *real,* truly *real,* was the small plane . . . the landing . . . the explosion. Explosion! My God . . . it exploded! My parents . . .

"Gillian! Gillian!" Gentle hands took her shoulders in an attempt to bring her back to the present, away from the agony that had suddenly gripped her pale features as it seized her mind. "I'm going to give you a mild sedative, Gillian. I want you to rest."

Eyes rounded, she pleaded hoarsely. "No . . . I can't rest. I have to know what happened."

The doctor's voice was soft yet firm. "Mrs. McCoy will stay with you. She'll be here all the time. We'll take it step by step. Now, please rest."

"You don't understand," she protested in a strained whisper. "I have to know . . ." Whether her strength fled before or after the sedative took effect was immaterial. Gillian fell into a deep sleep.

Several hours passed. Enmeshed in drug-induced slumber, she was oblivious to the excitement that surrounded her. Word of her awakening spread quickly through the floor. One by one, curious faces peered into her room, eager to see in live animation the one who had been so lovely in repose. Both hospital personnel and fellow patients had wondered long and hard about the young woman who, from the moment of her admission, even unconscious as she was, had been accorded VIP status. To be a guest of *the* Jeremy Dawson was no small thing!

When Gillian awoke, she found that Mrs. McCoy, her private nurse, was indeed by her side, jumping up the instant her eyes opened.

"Are you feeling better now, love? You went all tired on me before I could even get you that breakfast I promised. And here it's almost lunchtime," she clucked amiably. "No harm done. I'll bathe you and get you changed now. That'll perk you up a bit. All set?" No response was required. Gillian submitted to the woman's gentle ministrations as, preoccupied, she struggled to sift through her topsy-turvy thoughts. "There, now. Doesn't that feel better? There's nothing worse, I say, than feeling sticky. Such beautiful hair you have. We'll wash it tomorrow or the next day. In the meantime, I can brush it like I've been doing."

"Seven weeks? I've really been here for *seven weeks?*" It

was easier to talk now, her vocal chords finally beginning to respond to stimulation. Seven weeks—wasn't there to have been a show two weeks after she returned, a gallery opening soon after that, and numerous special orders to be filled in the meanwhile?

"Well, actually, you've only been *here* for six weeks. You spent a week in that other hospital."

"Other hospital?" A new twist.

"Why, in Vermont, love. Then Mr. Dawson brought you down to us." A perfectly acceptable explanation, from Mrs. McCoy's viewpoint. Not so from Gillian's.

"Mr. Dawson?"

Bypassing this seeming lack of recognition, the nurse babbled on, easing the clean blue nightgown over her patient's head. "Your Mr. Dawson is quite a gent, that he is. Coming down here every evening to see you. After working hard all day, too. Why, if it isn't here in Durham, it's in Raleigh, or Charleston, or even way out in some other part of the country. He's as close as we Tarheels get to a jet-setter, that one! But a loyal one he is, that man. Lucky *you* are to have him on your side!"

"Mr. Dawson?" There was no mistaking the bewilderment now, nor the vague look in Gillian's eye as she stared at the older woman.

"Your Mr. Dawson, love. He's been so—"

Gillian's tongue finally began to function at its normal speed. "I don't *know* anyone by the name of Dawson. And exactly what hospital *is* this?"

"Why, this is the Duke University Medical Center, love. But, then," she chided herself, "we forgot to tell you that, now, didn't we. And here you've been with us all these weeks!"

"The *Duke University* Medical Center?" Her eyes searched the room for a clue, then flew to the window. "But—but that's in North Carolina!"

"On the button! Durham, to be exact. Have you *never*

22

been in this neck of the woods before?" For the first time, the round face registered doubt.

With a forlorn shake of the head, Gillian sank back more deeply into the pillows. "What am I doing *here*? Why was I brought so far? Was there a special doctor . . . ?" It was beyond her comprehension that she should suddenly find herself such a distance from home.

Nurse McCoy, however, was momentarily preoccupied. "That's strange," she murmured, "I thought you had family in these parts. And Mr. Dawson certainly knew the color of your eyes, even *before* you'd opened them." Shaking her head absently, her attention returned to Gillian's quandary.

"Oh, your Mr. Dawson insisted you be brought. He lives nearby. And Dr. Worthin is an old friend of his. You know, we have a fine reputation—" she began, bent only on reassuring her charge.

"I know you do," Gillian interrupted in frustration. "But I have no idea why I was brought *here*. Surely, there were specialists closer—in Boston, New Haven, even New York?" The pitch of her voice had risen, reflecting her inner turmoil.

"Now, now, love. You're getting yourself all worked up. In time everything will be crystal clear. *He*'ll be by later today. You can ask him all the questions you want and I'm sure he'll be glad to give you all the answers. After all," she said with a murmur of mock contrition; "I'm only a *nurse* here. *He*'s the man who pulls the strings."

Gillian closed her eyes and turned her head to the side, away from the kind woman. Assailed by an emotional weakness as severe as that that seemed to have paralyzed her limbs, she could concentrate no longer. Spent by her mild exertion, she dozed off, to be brought back to consciousness by the aroma of a steaming lunch on the tray in the hands of the diligent Nurse McCoy. By the time the doctor stopped in to see her early that afternoon, Gillian had begun to wonder about the extent of her own physical injuries.

"What happened to me?" she asked timidly, feeling a wash of guilt at knowing that her parents had suffered the worst of the damage. Since she had learned of their loss, she'd known a pall of pain so pervasive that she absolutely had to divert her thoughts, if for no other reason than her own psychological survival. And survival seemed to be what these people around her had worked so hard for during the past seven weeks. Now it would be her own responsibility; she had to know what she faced.

Understanding this need, Peter Worthin stood close by her bedside. It disturbed him to see the intense sadness on her face, buried most deeply in the eyes, which now held his as she awaited his answer. Fortunately, he had good news to give on that score. It was truly, given the total destruction of the aircraft, a miracle.

"You were brought in with several broken ribs, a broken arm, and numerous deep gashes. I'm afraid"—he smiled apologetically—"that you've got several scars more than you had before." At her raised brow, he explained. "There was surgery to repair a lung that had been punctured by one of the ribs. You've got a nasty mark on your arm, which was also stitched before the bone was set"—he touched the skin of her upper arm, where, not quite hidden by the sleeve of her nightgown, peeped a jagged red slash—"and you've got another souvenir at your left temple, just beyond your hairline."

Instinctively, she reached up to touch her face, fingering the paper-thin ridge that extended for a good two inches beneath the wavy bangs that fell across her forehead.

"Oh, and one other small momento, I'm afraid, was a necessity. A tracheotomy was performed early on to help you breathe. It's a small gem—here, right at the hollow of your throat."

Her finger followed his in confirmation of this last battle

24

scar, before she let her arm fall back onto the bed. "Why do I feel so weak? It's an effort even to raise my hand."

"As I said before, Gillian, you've been through a lot. Your body has lain here, practically unused, for seven long weeks. A physical therapist has worked with you regularly, but it's a very different thing from actual exercise. Your muscles are greatly weakened, but they will come back quickly, given the proper care. You can hope to return to your work without a trace of a problem, once we're done with you. By now your bones have healed—you can see that you have no cast, no strappings—and it's mostly a matter of getting you up and about." He chuckled softly. "You've slept through the worst."

Humor, or appreciation of it, was beyond her reach at the moment. "What caused the unconsciousness—the gash on my head?"

He shrugged. "It could have been that or some other bang you took. When the plane exploded"—he noted the involuntary wince in his slim patient, but was determined to confront her little by little with the reality the investigators had been able to piece together—"you were thrown a distance."

Gillian's pallor added to the haunted cast of her eyes. In the long weeks during which he'd overseen her care, he'd often wondered what her soft features would look like wreathed in a smile. Sighing inwardly, he feared he still had a while to wait. With this emergence from her coma and her nearly healed body, the bulk of his official duty was done. Now it was a different sphere in which she needed help. "Would you like to talk about it, Gillian?"

She heard his voice, soft, kind, and beckoning, and struggled to comply. "I'd like to . . . but it's all so confusing . . . and frightening. There is so much I don't remember." Distress overshadowed her, clouding her blue eyes as it lent a quiver to her lips.

"That's understandable. Some of it may come back in

25

time. Other parts may be gone forever, due to that head injury. You're a very fortunate young woman to have awoken from a seven-week coma with as clear a mind as you have."

It was precisely that clear mind that suddenly demanded one particular answer. Her gaze was direct as she cornered him. "Who is this Mr. Dawson that Mrs. McCoy keeps mentioning?"

Having been occupied in another wing of the hospital since he'd last seen Gillian, the doctor had not spoken with Mrs. McCoy, now on her own lunch break, and had not heard of this seeming bit of amnesia. His sight narrowed as he studied his patient. "Jeremy? Jeremy Dawson?"

Gillian immediately detected his incredulity. "I don't remember any Jeremy Dawson. Should I?"

He hesitated a moment before answering, sorting things back in his own mind. "I was sure you had known him at one point. The name doesn't ring any bell?" She shook her head firmly, moments before a thread caught. There was some remotely familiar sound to the name, particularly since she'd heard his first. Yet she couldn't place it, try as she might, and was *sure* that she'd never consciously known anyone called Jeremy Dawson. She cast a skeptical eye at Dr. Worthin.

"Dawson is a fairly common name. In that sense, it sounds familiar—though not in terms of anyone I've ever known." Suddenly, a disturbing thought hit her. "Is it possible that I just can't *remember?* So many things about the . . . the accident . . . are fuzzy. Could this be tied up with that?"

Suspecting that his patient would overtire under such mental stress, the doctor reassured her softly. "Could be, though I doubt it. Your grasp on reality seems just fine. Please don't worry about it, Gillian. Okay?"

She had no choice. As he'd anticipated, the conversation had exhausted her, driving from her mind the many questions relating to this Jeremy Dawson's enigmatic presence in her life. Her voice was a mere whisper. "There's just so much I don't understand . . ." Closing her eyes once more, she followed her body's commands and drifted to sleep, oblivious of the sympathetic scrutiny the doctor gave her before he left the room.

No longer, however, was it the untroubled daze of unconsciousness. This sleep was dream-filled, playing itself out in steps, one superimposed on the other, in much the same manner as the silk-screen prints for which she'd become renowned. On the primary stencil was an image of herself with her parents, back in her childhood home in Boston, the three a close-knit group, tight, so tightly woven that nothing could penetrate. Cleared both of paint and glue, the silk next held an image of her mother's studio, where she'd first discovered her ability to draw, her teacher, patient and loving, standing at her shoulder. Stepping progressively, the stencil was of art school and an enthusiastic Gillian squeegeeing paint through the hardwood frame in her first print-making attempt. Subsequent stencils depicted her new home in Essex and her friends, who filled one void while leaving another untouched. There was a stencil tracing her emotional growth, boasting success, acclaim, and independence. There was one to capture a gentle reacquaintance, a plea, and a warning. And, finally, at the topmost layer of the work was a fiery mass of the craft that had carried her family on its last journey.

But when Gillian lifted her lids to the late afternoon sunlight, there was a different image in her mind. It was one that had no place here, for all of her imaginings. It was a fragment from the past, dredged up for no reason that her tortured mind could fathom. Yet it persisted, gold flecks burning out of dark brown eyes, searing a place in her memory for all time. He was dark, so very dark, with

27

black hair and sun-browned skin. He was tall, sturdy, and laden with mystery. He was silent, so silent, yet his presence was unmistakable. And his image stirred a note of warning within her. Magnetic yet forbidden, his saturnine features haunted her.

"There you are, love. Come back to visit us again?" Mrs. McCoy was at her elbow, smoothing her hair away from her warmed cheeks, fanning the chestnut tresses out upon the stark white of the pillow. "Now what would you be thinking of, love? That was a very strange look you woke up with!"

The dark image faded, relegated by will to its proper place in a faraway, forsaken past. "Strange?" she murmured hesitantly.

"Now, now. It was a *good* kind of strange, you know," the gentle smile assured her. "Let's get you sitting straight up for a change, love." Moving to the foot of the bed, she cranked up Gillian's head. "Mr. Dawson is sure to get a mechanized bed for you, now that we know you're awake to handle it. How's that? Good? Fine."

"Who *is* this Mr. Dawson?" Reminded abruptly of the mystery that had been far from solved by the doctor, Gillian clamped a hand on the softly inflated arm that now fluffed her pillows.

The woman's gray brows knit. "You really don't remember?" Gillian slowly shook her head. "Well, I guess there'll be lots of things you'll have forgotten. They'll come back." Hadn't Dr. Worthin said the same? Yet it was inconceivable to Gillian that she should owe so much of her care to a man whom she absolutely *did not know.*

"Who is he?" Her voice was less pointed, though insistent nonetheless.

"He's a wonderful fellow, your Mr. Dawson. He's been very good to you and very generous to the hospital."

"But who *is* he? What does he do? And what does he

28

have to do with me?" Born was an impatience, which was to mix with frustration and yield a raw crankiness.

"Why, he's very close to your family, so I was told. But you'll be able to ask him soon enough. He usually comes in just after dinner."

Gillian lay inert, frustrated by the repeatedly evasive responses she seemed to get on the subject of Jeremy Dawson. Silently she stewed at the audacity of some stranger to have claimed to be close to her family. She knew of *no one* by the name of Dawson. And despite the remote possibility that she did suffer selective amnesia, she felt certain that she recalled everything—everything, that is, up to the accident.

Her mind stumbled onto that agonizing memory. What had happened? They had landed safely, she thought. Why the—the explosion? Had the impact been that great? Why hadn't her parents escaped the aircraft as she had?

"Why was I brought *here?* Why all the way *here?*" She felt desperately alone and puzzled.

"He'll explain, love."

"My parents—were they buried?" A hollow at the core of her rib cage gnawed torturously.

"Now, now, everything has been taken care of. Your fellow will be along to answer anything else. Be patient, love."

Exasperated, Gillian sat forward, snapping with a spark she'd doubted she could produce, "He's not my 'fellow.' I don't know the man! And I wish there was someone who would answer me now!"

"Now that's a very good sign. You've moved on your own! It must feel odd after all these weeks. My, but I'm real proud of you, I am!" The cherubic face beamed down at her, deliberately ignoring the show of temper. Gillian sank back against the bed with a tired sigh, resigned to save her strength for the appearance of the omnipotent Mr. Dawson.

It was the helplessness of her situation that struck her strongly. Here she lay, weak and bedridden, unable to recall the most immediate past, unable to comprehend the present, unable to envision the future. Helplessness was an alien trait to her, a child born with a budding and independent spirit. She'd always been an eager and enthusiastic learner, latching on to an idea, then following it, often pushing it, to its ultimate conclusion. She'd always been bent on controlling her own destiny—choosing her friends, her clothes, her studies, her avocation—all this in defiance of her parents' more protective instincts, particularly in one realm.

In the matter of the opposite sex, Gillian's parents had been unrelentingly rigid. As their daughter's outstanding good looks became even more so, attracting any number of admiring schoolboys, they guarded her closely, discouraging her from involvements whenever possible, offering any number of primitive caveats. By the time she'd reached high school, she'd thoroughly ingested a distrust of men, which would be mitigated only when, once in college, she had freer access to this touted evil.

Promiscuous she could never be, given the deep-seated thread of fear that had been so successfully instilled. She was a quiet and introspective person, unabashedly dedicated to her art. Yet, as one would have expected of a beautiful young woman, she dated frequently, through college and after, particularly once she'd escaped the over-watchful eye of her parents. Though she'd often wondered at the cause of such extreme views in these otherwise easygoing people, she'd never pursued it. She'd loved her parents and had accepted the fact that, with an only child and no extended family to speak of, her parents had merely erred on the side of too much care.

As for Gillian, marriage had never held a major role in her life's scheme, though in recent years she'd come to know a particular void in her life—one that she hadn't had

30

the courage yet to fill. Rather, she'd delved deeper into the world of art, satisfying herself with the innocence of close companionship and pleasant camaraderie, both female and male, which sketched, painted, and printed its way in and about the North Shore of Massachusetts.

It had been her hope that, living away from her parents as she did, they would finally relax on the matter of men. Surely they might even realize that, at the age of twenty-seven, she was fully capable of handling her own affairs. It had indeed been a shock, at that last opening, when the old warning had been resurrected—blunt, chilling, and seemingly unwarranted.

Just as . . . just as . . . her memory jogged back to the warning. . . the warning had come so unexpectedly . . . in those last few seconds . . . before . . . before . . .

A shaft of misery speared her. That warning—what had her father actually said? Despite her searchings, she could not recall the words, or whether, in fact, she had legitimately heard them. Yet a warning rumbled within her, one distinctly associated with the moments before the explosion. Unbidden, a dark and mysterious visage sprang up in her mind, a stark throwback to the earlier warning that had prompted that same despairing tone.

Once again she dozed off, taking the surest escape from her turmoil. Awakening somewhat more relaxed, she was fussed over and fed by the ever-catering Nurse McCoy before the latter left for the night with a final monologue of promises of activity on tomorrow's agenda.

If Gillian had hoped for more quiet time to ponder her dilemma, she had underestimated the enthusiasm for her very condition. From the moment of Mrs. McCoy's departure, as though the woman had been a guard at the door now suddenly removed, there was a stream of visitors, no more than one or two at a time, none staying longer than a few minutes, though all determined to welcome her, to comment on her miraculous recovery, and—to her growing consternation—to shower compliments on her apparent guardian, the elusive Jeremy Dawson.

For elusive was the term Gillian had quickly come to associate with this mystery man. Despite the frequency of his name on the lips of all around her, she had seen hide nor hair of him. As early evening waned to social history, he had not appeared. Hadn't Mrs. McCoy said he came by each evening? Then where was he? She was tired now, exhausted by the psychological activity of the day, and this fatigue had only aggravated her sense of loss, confusion, and frustration. She was cranky, fuming inwardly against this man who kept her waiting. It was in this irascible frame of mind that she fell asleep, shortly before ten, resigned to the postponement of this much heralded visit. She had most definitely underestimated Jeremy Dawson.

It was well after eleven that the door to her room opened, allowing the night lights of the corridor to meld with the dim dresser lamp earlier left aglow. He had come as soon as he'd received the message, unfortunately a mere twenty minutes before, having been out of the state on business for the day. If only he'd arrived sooner, he might have caught her awake! After all these weeks, who would have thought she'd have regained consciousness with as much lucidity as Peter reported he'd found!

Slowly, leaving the door ajar, he entered the room, walking quietly toward the bed on which she lay, her slender arms draped, one across her body, one bent up by her head, in a pose of slumber that the night nurse could never have created. Her pale features, lit ever so gently by the soft light in the room, were much as they'd been in the past, save a hint of disturbance that tensed her brow.

"Is that you, Mr. Dawson?" The voice was loud from the door behind him, typical of the odd disregard all night supervisors seemed to hold for the sleeping.

The dark form turned, in mild irritation, toward the sound, his own tone an infinitely soft, deep hum. "Yes, Miss Oberman. Was there something you wanted?"

In contrast to his near whisper, the nurse appeared to bellow. "Oh, no, sir. I was just startled. We hadn't expected you so late."

Annoyed as much by her interference as by the continued loudness of her voice, he retraced his steps to the door, clenching his fist in a bid for patience. It had been a long, tiring day. And he had not stopped by at the hospital to give a schedule rundown to Oberman. "I won't be but a moment. We wouldn't want to wake the patient, now, would we?" His blatant mockery was enough, mercifully, to send the nurse back to her station with a somber headshake. His warning, however, was too late.

Stirred from slumber by the voices, one loud and distinctly institutional, the other barely audible, though clearly masculine, Gillian slowly opened her eyes just as the tall figure turned back to her. Standing just inside the door and highly backlit as he was, she could make no identification other than the most gross physical one. This was a man tall and slim, broader of shoulder than hip, with a stance that proclaimed command over all. Intuitively, Gillian knew this to be the man she had awaited in vain all evening. It would be none other than Jeremy Dawson.

Soft, easy strides brought him toward her. If his day had been a trying one, hers could be considered no less. As the events of the day backed up on her—a brutal amalgam of fear, confusion, and grief—she grew distinctly testy. Shorn both of rationality and justification, she was about to hold this mysterious Mr. Dawson responsible for her every woe. Pulse racing in anticipation, she was in no way prepared, however, for what the spreading cast of light, as he approached, would reveal.

Emerging, step by step, from the darkness, his features

slowly crystallized. In the final instant an emotional vise seized her middle, forcing from her lips an involuntary gasp. His hair was as black as ever, his skin as bronzed. His eyes were a mosaic of gold on brown, his straight nose a symbol of strength. In her confusion she might have doubted the truth of her vision—until he smiled, a smile broad and slightly askew, revealing to her that singly endearing dimple on his right cheek, which she'd caught hint of but once before.

"Hi, Jill." His voice was, indeed, the croon of her dreams, his hand, as the backs of his strong fingers ran so lightly down her cheek, the hand of her fragmented imaginings. Identified, at last, was the scent, a distinct mingling of musk, man, and menthol, a link from the past into the present. Recognition was achieved—all that remained was an explanation.

It was a hoarse whisper, a cross between question of disbelief and statement of astonishment, which signaled her full awakening. "Jed?"

CHAPTER 2

"Jed?" It had to be repeated to be believed, and even then she was doubtful.

"It's me, Jill." The whiteness of his smile glittered during the long moments he stood looking down at her. It took an enormous effort on his part to soft-pedal his excitement at seeing her awake. And yes, aware—she'd recognized him immediately. "How do you feel?" What sounded banal was among the uppermost thoughts in his mind.

Her blue-eyed gaze, though clouded with confusion, held his. "Weird," she answered softly. "I don't understand *any* of this. What are *you* doing here?" Her incipient anger, hovering mere moments before, had vanished in the face of this man whom she'd never thought to see again. That she saw him now, after so many long months, standing majestically, tall and straight, beside her, compounded her bewilderment.

Unfazed, he reached over to take her hand in his. "I'm visiting *you!* We've all been on pins and needles, waiting and wondering. You look terrific with your eyes open for a change!"

As had been the case earlier that day, humor was beyond her. "Why are you here?" At the moment her mind was strictly one-tracked. "How did you know I was here?"

Pondering his approach, he temporarily evaded the issue. "Do you mind if I sit? It's been one hell of a day!" Without a thought, she made a faint move to ease over on the bed, allowing him to sit on its edge. It hadn't occurred to her that he would sit further away, on a chair; it was perfectly natural that, as the only familiar face she knew

35

in these strange circumstances, he should remain close to her. Lord only knew that the hospital mattress was hard enough to preclude all but the slightest tilt under his weight!

He had neither taken his eyes from hers nor released her hand as he sat down. And she had neither the strength nor the will to look away. It was as it had been before—an awesome visual magnetism that bound her inexplicably to him. Their relationship had been a nonrelationship; they had shared so much, yet so little.

Studying her in the soft light, Jed felt an overwhelming compassion. She'd lost so much, nearly lost more. How was she holding up? That she was confused was obvious. If only he'd spoken to Pete before he'd come; then he would have had a better idea of what she knew and what she didn't. By all indications, she was as yet unaware of his involvement.

"I'm sorry that I didn't get here sooner," he began carefully, "but I've been out of the state all day. I only got Pete's message a few minutes ago."

"Pete?" For some reason, all connections eluded her.

"Peter Worthin, your doctor."

"Do *you* know him, too?" His automatic use of the doctor's first name suggested an acquaintance beyond the professional one. Could it be that Jed was a close friend of Dr. Worthin's, just as was this Jeremy Dawson?

He nodded. "Pete and I have been close friends since college. We both studied at the university here."

Searching her memory, Gillian could find no recollection of the fact that Jed had spent time in North Carolina. She'd assumed him to be a northerner, more of a local along with the other patrons of the Essex art shows. But then, she really knew nothing about him. Suddenly, she was back to square one. Yet the comfort of his touch, the unexpected appearance of this compelling man, gave her a patience she'd lacked earlier.

"You've got to help me, Jed," she pleaded softly. "There's so much that I don't follow, and I can't seem to get any straight answers from the people around here. They keep telling me to wait, that things will come back to me, that everything will be crystal clear in time. In the meanwhile, I just lie here totally disoriented." In spite of herself, a certain frantic note had escaped in her plea. She was unaware of the remarkable force with which her hand clutched his now.

Jed saw her distress. "Take it easy, now, angel. You seem frightened. There's no reason to be." He reached to smooth the hair back from her face, gently tracing the scar at her temple with his forefinger. For a split second, she forgot all but the touch of his hand, the endearment he'd used, the reassuring tone of his voice. She felt no more than a child, comforted by a grown-up. Yet she was no child, and this was not just any grown-up. This was Jed, whom she'd bumped into at one art show after the other. This was Jed, who, in public amid her friends and parents, had reached for her with a startling visual touch. And some small voice reminded her that this was the Jed who had disconcerted her father so strangely.

Brought to the present by this chilling memory, she explained. "I'm not frightened—just confused. I have no idea what I'm doing here, at *this* medical center, when the accident happened in Vermont. I have no idea what *you*'re doing here, especially when I haven't seen you since last fall. And I have no idea who this Jeremy Dawson is—he seems to have been responsible for bringing me here, and everyone around here knows the man, but I have *no idea* who he is!" Breathless at the exertion, she awaited his response.

Even in the dimness of the night light, the amber flames shot brightly from his eyes, bespeaking a mix of doubt and faint amusement. "You have *no idea,*" he echoed softly, "who Jeremy Dawson is?"

37

"None whatsoever!"

"Are you sure?" There was something in his tone, a subtle thread of laughter, that caught her up. Obviously he knew something she did not.

Puzzled, she shook her head. "I'm positive that the name means nothing to me. I've tried to remember . . . but I . . ." She looked away finally, struggling, searching anew.

Taking pity on her, Jed ended the misunderstanding. "Jill, *I* am Jeremy Dawson. I thought you knew." He honestly had; he'd been mistaken. "Jed is a nickname I've had since I was a child—the acronym of my full name. I grew up as Jed, using Jeremy only in college and after. Jed is more personal; I guess I'll always think of myself as Jed. That's why I originally introduced myself to you as Jed." Astounded, she missed the subtle significance of the last. It was enough for her to assimilate the fact that this Jed, a most vital ghost from her past, was the Jeremy Dawson of her present.

Her brows knit. "*You're* Jeremy Dawson?" At his nod of confirmation, she continued, her voice holding a tremor he'd not noticed before. To look at her, particularly knowing what she'd been through physically, she'd seemed recovered. Perhaps, though, she was weaker than she looked. "Then you're the one who brought me here." It was a whisper reaffirming what she already knew. "But why?" That she didn't know.

"It seemed the most sensible thing, given the circumstances."

His answer explained nothing. Gillian tried again. "But it makes *no* sense to me. The accident was in Vermont. There are any number of fine hospitals in New England. Why all the way down here?"

As the doctor and nurse had done in turn, Jed now tasted a bit of the confusion that dominated her wakefulness. Surely she would see the reasoning. Sighing, he began slowly. "You were alone . . . after the accident."

"I know that my parents died, if that's what you're hedging at." She made the statement without a flinch, the core of her attention diverted by her present quandary. "But that doesn't explain why I'm *here.*"

"We thought it best, since you had no one there. I wanted to supervise your medical care myself; this was the best place to do that."

"Wait a minute. No one there? Everyone I know *is* back home," she argued desperately. "I have friends, fellow artists. I have a roommate. I have agents, teachers, clients. There are many people I have there. It's *here* that I have no one."

"You have me."

How simple his statement, yet heart stopping. Even amid her perplexity, she felt its effect. At another time, the words would have carried her to unknown heights; now they merely carried her to the unknown. Doggedly she pursued the latter. "That's what I don't understand. How did you even find out about the accident? And why did you become involved? You owe me nothing. We mean nothing to one another. Why, Jed? Why?" It had all come back, and she felt the pain of disappointment once again. He had vanished—simply disappeared from the art scene. He'd missed her last two openings, had never made any further effort to contact her. Why? True, they'd never seen each other outside of an art gallery; they'd exchanged few words. Yet she'd instinctively felt they'd communicated in other, deeper ways. Why had he severed the contact? Hadn't he been the one to initiate it? Why had he let her down at those last two openings, when she'd come to anticipate his presence as much as the showing itself? Why?

Vulnerability was written over her wan features. Although unaware of her train of thought, his was much on the same track. He felt something special, as he had from the start, for this beautiful young woman. In the instant, he truly believed that she had no knowledge of the connection in North Carolina. Could that be possible? Or was it merely a denial, psychologically induced and related to the stress she must have felt on this day. Whatever the cause of her shortcoming, he felt it his duty to confront her.

"Jill," he began, quietly and calmly, "I brought you here, among other reasons, at the request of your grandmother."

My God, what next? "Grandmother?" Whatever was he talking about?

"She was notified, as your only surviving relative, soon after the accident. She wanted you closer to her."

"My grandmother?" she breathed incredulously. "My only surviving relative?"

Jed took in her rounded eyes, moist lips, and now visibly trembling hand. "You *do* know your grandmother, don't you?" Was it possible she'd been kept in the dark all these years? If not, she was an actress of the highest caliber.

It was a rerun of an earlier tape, one in which she'd claimed no knowledge of a Jeremy Dawson. Gillian was floored by this new information, of which she'd had no prior inkling. "This is absurd, Jed. I have no grandmother. Both of my parents' parents died before I was born. I haven't *got* a grandmother." Perhaps if she repeated it, it would be true. Regardless of how comforting it would have been to have had such a person by her side through this ordeal, she somehow felt the need to cling to the familiar, the status quo. Desperate to retain her grasp on reality, she tightened her grasp on Jed's hand without even realizing it.

On his part, Jed simmered. How could her parents have done this to her? How could they have deprived her, for so many years, of an aging woman who had so much love

40

to give? How could they have deprived that woman of her granddaughter? How could they have held a lonely woman responsible, these many long years, for what had been out of her hands at the time?

Gillian watched as Jed's jaw, straight and bold, tensed. Misinterpreting his fury, she cowered beneath the features, suddenly so harsh, so angry. It seemed that he didn't believe her. How could he imagine her denying her own grandmother, had she known of her existence? Instantly, she felt a dire need to escape all of this. Closing her eyes, she turned her head away. "I think I'd like to sleep now." Her battered emotions had reached their limit; at the moment, she could think no more.

She'd not closed her eyes before he'd seen their pain. Jed ached for her; she'd been through so much. To have this added burden, this new concept to digest along with the others that she'd awakened to, after seven weeks of oblivion . . . Could she accept it all? Yes, he ached for her, in a totally different way than he had from the moment he'd first laid eyes on her, even without her knowledge, so many years ago.

Once again he stroked her hair, a poor substitute for the comforting embrace he would have preferred, yet the only one he dared, given her distressed state and its cause. After all, he'd been a major instrument in so much of her present turmoil. His voice was gentle, a reassuring croon. "That might be best. You need time to adjust to everything. I'll drop by in the morning to see you. How's that?"

Part of Gillian wanted to refuse him, to deny both his claim and his presence, to accuse him of wrongful interference in bringing her, against her knowledge and without her permission, to this unfamiliar place. She wanted to demand he return her to Boston, then to her home in Essex, where perhaps things might once again be the same. But in her heart she knew they never would be. Her life had been irrevocably altered by that tragic accident

41

that had taken her parents from her. No, things would never be the same. And, in light of that reality, she needed Jed as her sole link to another life. She needed his presence, and the strength he'd always seemed to possess, to ease her over what promised to be a charm of mystery.

He spoke no more, merely ran the length of a strong finger along her cheek. When she'd composed herself enough to open her eyes, he was gone, silent as a mountain lion stealing off into the night. An incongruous smile ghost-touched her lips as she realized that he'd never awaited, nor expected, an answer to his question. It mattered not whether she desired his company; if he was so inclined, he would be by her side in the morning.

For a long time she lay awake, striving to accept both Jeremy Dawson and this grandmother whose existence he'd announced. It was preposterous; she could make neither head nor tail of it. Her thoughts chased circles around themselves, each beginning and ending with a pair of gold-flecked brown eyes. It was amid this eddy that she fell asleep, determined to resume her battle in the morning.

Unfortunately, she had little time for quiet thought. For Mrs. McCoy was at her bedside, bright and early as dictated by hospital custom, intent on bathing and grooming her before breakfast. And, as much as she would like to have begun to do some of these things for herself, she felt sufficiently weak to allow the robust woman to pamper her. Gillian refrained from mentioning her midnight visitor to the concerned nurse, hesitant to get into a discussion when her feelings were still so raw. The nurse, however, was fully aware of Jeremy Dawson's visit, raising the issue in passing herself. Actually, Gillian could not have shared her feelings had she wanted to, so awesome a task would it have been to interrupt the woman's animated babbling.

Following breakfast was a visit by the doctor, making his rounds in the company of a handful of others at varying professional levels. She was the main attraction of the day, a curiosity for all to see. Her interaction with Dr. Worthin, though pleasant, was strictly medical, giving her no opportunity, or privacy, to discuss her dilemma with him. On the heels of this attentive crew came the therapist, introducing herself and running through some preliminary exercises before helping Gillian out of bed. Wobbly as her knees felt, it was hard for her to grasp the fact that she'd been off her feet for so many weeks, despite the excitement brimming in those all around at her every new move.

To Nurse McCoy the most important thing seemed to be to get her to the solarium for a breath of fresh air and a bit of sun. "It's been so long, love, and you've missed the first part of the summer altogether. The change of scenery will do you wonders." Gillian grimaced. Since she'd awoken from her coma a mere twenty-four hours before, she'd seen one change of scenery, so to speak, after the other. All she wanted was some peace and quiet to assimilate it all. But, she reasoned, if Mrs. McCoy was so determined that she go to the solarium, she'd seek her peace and quiet there. Arguing was beyond her with this well-intentioned whirlwind of a woman.

"Now, love," said the energetic nurse by her side, "let's get you sitting up and I'll help you on with the lovely robe that matches your nightie. Ah, doesn't the apricot look delicious!" It was a different nightgown she wore and a new robe that she soon found gliding about her shoulders. The folds of both were loose and caftanesque, the nightgown of a lighter, more delicate fabric, sleeveless and V-necked, with the robe wide sleeved over it. Gingerly she fingered the smooth fabric, wondering at the generosity of the man she knew as Jed. "Beautiful, isn't it?" Mrs. McCoy cooed, adjusting the shoulders to her satisfaction.

"Ummmm," Gillian murmured thoughtfully. It was, indeed, both beautiful and understated, as was her way. He'd chosen well, much as she might have done had she

43

purchased the outfit herself. Unfortunately, she never would have considered spending the amount of money that this set must have cost him. Grateful as she was, there was an odd sense of annoyance that ruffled her. She hadn't wanted to be indebted to any man, particularly one who mystified her as much as did Jeremy Dawson.

"You sit right here, love, and don't move a muscle." The bubbling wonder interrupted her thoughts. "I'm off to commandeer a wheelchair for us. You'll ride to that solarium in grand style."

"Indeed she will," a deep voice drawled from the door, pulling both female heads up and around with a start. Gillian could not help but catch her breath. Seeing him the night before, in the near darkness, she'd been overwhelmed primarily by his sudden reappearance in her life. Now, however, with that initial fact accomplished, she was stunned anew by his magnificence, much as she had been at each of those encounters in Essex.

Lounging casually against the doorjamb with his arms crossed jauntily over his chest, he was the image of self-assurance. A lightweight gray business suit fit his tall frame with a made-to-order slimness; a white shirt set off his dark features dramatically. But those features—those features were handsome beyond belief, a fine blend of the rugged mountain man and the aristocrat. Gillian absorbed it all, her pulse certain to be found racing, were the good doctor to measure it then. She savored his virile flair, even as her eyes remained fixed on his in silent interaction such as she'd never known with any other person.

Jed was pleased to have arrived at such an opportune time, when he'd have the excuse to do something he'd long wanted to do. Disengaging his form from the doorjamb, he approached the bed in long, easy strides.

"Why, Mr. Dawson! How nice to see you so early." Mercifully, Mrs. McCoy found her tongue—rarely displaced, never lost—before Gillian's tongue-tied state was made apparent, and with the resident chatterer now in action, the latter happily remained silent. "I understand you were by last night for a bit. How thoughtful of you, after such a long day! You're just in time to see how lovely this pretty miss looks today!"

To her immediate dismay, Gillian blushed. If she'd realized that the nurse would be making such statements, she would have made the effort to divert the conversation. Jed, however, was pleased at the show of color—as pleased as he was at the sight of her so splendidly gowned. He made no comment, however, though his eyes spoke his thoughts as he gazed into hers. The communication was deep and instantaneous, yet she had no warning for what he was to do next.

Before she realized what was happening, he had slipped a strong arm behind her back and another beneath her knees and had scooped her into his arms. "Hang on, angel," he whispered, for her ears alone, as he wisked her out of the room, down the corridor, and into a large, thoroughly transparent room. She was to later reflect on her distraction during the short trip, remembering nothing of the long corridor that she'd never seen and that should have therefore interested her. At the time, however, her senses reeled from the sheer masculinity of the man who held her, the strength and sureness that his every step proclaimed. She'd unconsciously put an arm around his neck when he'd first lifted her; slowly she became aware of the warm vitality of the dark hair that had been neatly trimmed to end just there. Her arm was the last thing to leave him when he set her down, slowly and gently, on the padded chaise. There were a scattering of other patients in the room, though hardly a sound came from any of them. Indeed, it was the chorus of the birds, chirping gleefully through the open screens, that broke the silence quite pleasantly.

For an instant, warmed by the sun, serenaded by the

birds, and in the company of this unusually spectacular man, Gillian forgot all else but the sheer loveliness of the moment. For an instant, she felt carefree and relaxed. For an instant, she felt totally content. Only for an instant. In the next, she recalled how and why she had come to be here, and the aura of unhappiness slithered over her once more.

Having caught that peaceful instant and its disappearance, Jed pulled a chair up close beside her. "Comfortable?"

"Uh-huh."

"Feeling any better this morning?"

"Some."

"Are you angry with me?" Small talk was not his favorite, she mused; but then, neither was it hers! If it was business he wanted, business he'd get.

She answered him head-on, doing the thinking aloud that she'd hoped to do privately. "Angry, no. Puzzled, yes."

He smiled gently. "Now why should I puzzle you. Haven't I been honest with you? When you've asked a question, I believe I've given you an answer."

"That you have. But your answers are so very difficult to believe. And there are so many other questions I haven't even asked yet."

Jed could not help but sit back and admire the picture before him. There she lay, a wisp of apricot on a bed of lemon, her hands folded gracefully in her lap, the pallor of her skin framed artfully by the long chestnut fall that cascaded about her shoulders and cushioned her head against the back of the chaise. He'd correctly dubbed her an angel, for she seemed, in that pose, both pure and innocent. He marveled at the inner strength that enabled her to sit so calmly and systematically voice her thoughts to him. It was the same inner strength he'd seen so often in another—the woman who was rightfully her grandmother.

"Where would you like to begin?" he asked as calmly.

Regarding him as he sat, leaning toward her, elbows resting on his knees, fingers locked together, Gillian felt a surge of trust and intimacy. "My . . . grandmother. Tell me about her. If there is such a relative, I know nothing of her."

It was an easy subject to warm to. "She is a remarkable woman, I'd say now in her late seventies, though no one seems to know for sure. Rural record-keeping is as casual as the people themselves!"

Gillian interrupted to backtrack. "My father was originally from Rhode Island. It was my mother who was from the south. She never completely lost her twang, though I'm sure she worked at it." A grin surfaced for the moment as she recalled that only in those most rare occurrences when her mother lost her temper had the accent been noticeable. "So it is on my mother's side, this . . . grandmother of mine." The title came strangely to her lips, reflecting her persistent doubt as to its legitimacy.

"Yes. Her name is Amalia Cartwright." For good reason, he paused.

"Cartwright?" That had been her mother's maiden name, though only the initial had ever appeared between the Sarah and the Montgomery. If Jed's claim was a hoax, this was surely a coincidence.

"Her husband's name was Josiah. He died several years ago. They had two children—a daughter, then a son. Your mother was that daughter."

Almost against her will, Gillian found herself becoming progressively involved in the story. "Whatever happened to the brother?" Hadn't Jed described her grandmother as her only living relative?

"The brother was younger by several years. Your mother and he were very close; she was like a second mother to him. I understand she was that way." Gillian had firsthand evidence of this, having had a taste of her mother's potential for overprotectiveness. "He died in Korea, shortly before you were born. He was an officer, a career man." Jed grimaced; he'd never understood why Sarah Cartwright hadn't returned even for the funeral. Her absence, much as it might have eased tension on one score, had added to Amalia's pain.

Gillian felt a strange sorrow. She had to know more. "What was his name?" she prodded timidly, her soft gaze darting through the thick fringe of eyelashes toward Jed's.

His expression grew momentarily taut. "Giles." Gillian's mother had refused to attend the funeral, yet she'd named her only child after her dead brother. It was very sad, he mused, for families to carry such bitterness for so long. The only redeeming thought he could muster was that Sarah Montgomery, much as her mother before her, had been at the powerless end of a very old-fashioned marriage. If this was true, he could think of very little good to say for Gillian's father. But then, on that score, he was already biased. As wrong as it was to think ill of the dead, he doubted he could forgive Tom Montgomery for having kept so very much from Gillian. She had a right to know—about everything.

This coincidence of the names was slightly harder for Gillian to swallow. Giles—Gillian. Had she been named after the uncle who died shortly before her birth? She'd assumed, all these years, that her parents had chosen the name simply because they liked it!

"Where does . . . she . . . live now?" Uncertainty crept into her voice.

"Amalia lives in the western part of the state. She has a lovely home just beyond Black Mountain."

The lush green of the foliage, blooming gaily throughout the grounds of the medical center, drew Gillian's attention. The cultured wildness of it conjured up images of

48

that part of the state she knew, from geography studies alone, would be more rugged. "Black Mountain?" she echoed, testing the words on her tongue for some—any—familiarity. Her mother, now that she thought about it, had evaded most talk of her early home and upbringing. Believing that such discussions brought back the pain of remembering parents long dead, Gillian had never prodded. Now, for the first time, she wondered whether there had indeed been great pain in her mother's memory, but pain of an entirely different source.

A slow relaxation softened Jed's features. This was the land he loved; his mind fled to it willingly. "Your grandmother is one of the great ladies of the Blue Ridge Mountains. She knows well the rolling hills, the forested high country, and the purple mist that can cast its spell. Your grandfather, in the end, did quite well financially, yet he could never coax your grandmother to leave her beloved woodland."

His words were enchanting, striking a chord in Gillian that beckoned, if only to satisfy the artist in her. Her immediate thoughts, however, were more pointed. "Then she hasn't been here to visit me?"

Hauled abruptly back from the mountains to the core of civilization, Jed shifted his position, crossing one long leg over the other as he leaned back in his seat. Gillian felt her eyes drawn to the pull of fabric across a muscled thigh; chagrined, she tore her eyes away and back to his face. The frown there gave her a moment's fright, until she heard its cause in the ensuing words.

"She hasn't been well in recent years. It's difficult for her to get around. She did come to visit when you first arrived. The trip tired her, though. She's been unable to get back to Durham since. Actually, I urged her not to come, with you in a coma and unaware of her presence."

A fleeting image of kind words and gentle hands returned. Gillian wondered whether she had, in fact, been aware of more than they'd thought. She knew now that it had been Jed's presence that had sifted through to her consciousness. Had there been another? Suddenly she wondered about the connection between the two.

"How do you know all this, Jed? What is your relationship with this woman you claim is my grandmother? You seem very devoted to her." Nervously, she studied her tapered fingernails, tracing the tips of each on her left hand with her right thumb. "Are we related in some far-fetched way?" Eyes downcast, she prayed that this was not the case.

Jed laughed, throwing his head back as much in relief from tension as in genuine good humor. "Not by a long shot, thank goodness!" Then, thinking aloud, he sobered. "If you'd been related to me, you would have known about Amalia years ago. You would have known *everything*. It was cruel to have kept the two of you from each other."

Gillian bristled on behalf of her parents. "That's unfair. My parents aren't here to defend themselves against your claim. And I'm not even sure *I* believe you." The blue of her eyes hardened in the strongest show of spirit she'd made since her awakening. It was a good sign, Jed mused, his mind wandering helplessly to the creamy cast the sun gave her skin.

"You will," he murmured absently. Of that he was convinced.

Gillian wasn't so sure. Amid the sparks of a budding rebellion, she took him on. "How can you know that? This whole story is pretty bizarre, when you get down to it. I feel as though I'm a victim in some great mystery, looking desperately for clues. I haven't seen any proof of what you've suggested. And who *are* you, anyway? What is your connection to this whole thing? You still haven't given me a direct answer to that one!"

Undaunted by her barrage, he leaned forward once again. "I've known your grandmother since I was a child.

50

In many ways she was the mother I never had, though she was older than my own would have been." Once more, Gillian was made sharply aware of how little she knew about the man before her.

"Your mother—when did she die?"

His jaw tensed. "She didn't die. She left. It seems that mountain life was too much for her." Much as he tried, he could not completely hide the bitterness he still felt. Realizing this, he deftly shifted the focus of the conversation back to safer ground. "At any rate, I had Amalia. She was always there for me to talk with. She's a marvelous woman, with plenty of love to give—if given the chance." The last was spoken with a definite edge, his eyes underscoring it with intensity.

But Gillian had become preoccupied with a very disturbing thought. "If this grandmother of mine is so wonderful, why would my parents have kept her identity from me?" She was suddenly aware of a strange nagging in the furthermost reaches of her mind and assumed this prolonged conversation to have caused a nascent headache. Determinedly she ignored it.

"That's something I can't say, Jill." He had some pretty solid theories on the matter, yet he wondered whether he'd ever be able to share them with her. She had been kept ignorant of so very much!

Gillian would have been the first to agree with him. Persistently, she prodded further. "Then let's concentrate on what we—or, more accurately, you—*can* say. Am I correct in assuming that you acted as an agent of my . . . grandmother . . . in bringing me here?"

"Yes."

The vague sense of disappointment she felt at his summary response was quickly compensated for by a spurt of forcefulness. "And will I have an opportunity to meet my . . . grandmother . . . before I leave this hospital to return to Essex?"

A nerve tensed within Jed, urging him to choose his words carefully. "You'll meet her soon."

Gillian felt a sense of foreboding she could not understand. It was as though the grip on her own life, which she had had so firmly in the past, then lost temporarily in the wake of the accident, was bound to elude her. Summoning her final shreds of strength, she confronted him. "Soon I'll be going home. There doesn't seem to be that much wrong with me that a little work won't cure. I'd like to go back up north as soon as possible. Will you arrange that, too?" The last was added with a note of sarcasm she hadn't intended. Only then did she realize that she resented having become so suddenly and totally dependent.

Momentarily taken aback, he sent her a cool glare. Then, in an abrupt turn, his gaze softened. In the instant, he found himself regarding no longer the ill young woman he'd brought here, but the beautiful one he'd remembered so vividly. She was so vulnerable, so appealing; his eyes darkened with a long-dormant emotion.

"I can arrange most anything," he drawled softly.

The sudden alteration of both his tone and the look in his eyes startled her. He was close—so very close that she could smell the scent that was unique to him, that blend of man and tobacco that had been imprinted on her memory bank. In a wave of sensation, she relived those past moments of attraction, electrical and new, never pursued.

Silently, his dark gaze magnetized her, locking her into a depth of communication more heady than anything she'd remembered. Instantly, all resentment and frustration, confusion and unsureness were forgotten. She became oblivious to all around her save the compelling man whose head now lowered slowly to hers. Instinctively, her lips parted to meet his, to taste that which she'd only imagined in fevered dreams.

Imagination yielded to reality. His firm lips feather-touched hers, barely touching, yet creating a well of excitement within her that threatened to freely bubble over. Then, for a devastating instant, he drew back. Gold flecks sent a beam of warmth to her very core, as his eyes held hers. When slowly his mouth regained its possession, now in full, a throbbing kiss, she trembled in delight. Never, never had she been kissed as passionately; never, never had she responded likewise. It was a Gillian she'd never known existed—one who gave herself over willingly to the joys of womanhood, the great unknown that she'd been taught to fear.

Yet as his lips coaxed and caressed hers, exploring each curve and tilt of her pliant mouth, fear was the furthest thing from her mind. Her every touchpoint tingled under the sensual assault launched by his kiss. When he pulled away, she was left breathless and bereft.

His voice, deep and husky, added another heady element to the mountain of sensation that had risen, volcano fashion, from the steady level of the sea. "I should have arranged *that* much sooner. It was long overdue."

Dazedly, she gazed at the crooked smile that brought out his dimple, a dimple with a hint of the devil in it now. To her astonishment, he straightened in his seat, then stood up. "And I'm afraid I'm long overdue myself. I was expected at the office an hour ago. See you tonight?"

Speechless, Gillian sat motionless as the back of his hand skimmed her cheek, then watched as he casually leaned over to place a brotherly kiss on the shiny chestnut crown of her head. With no more than a handful of long steps, he was at the door and into the corridor. Stunned, she followed his tall frame as it ambled steadily on, shortly to round a corner and be lost from view.

In a flash, a torrent of fury engulfed her. How could he have done that? How could he have seduced her so successfully, then simply turned off the sensual button? Placing a shaky finger to her heated lips, she recalled again the fiery touch of his—and fury changed to shame. Whatever was she doing? Whatever had come over her? How could she have let herself go like that? They'd been in the midst of a critical discussion, one concerning her very future. Yet she'd let him shut her up with a mere kiss! And, to make matters even worse, she'd been angry that he'd ended it! A mere kiss—it was inexcusable!

But that mere kiss was on his mind also. As the elevator glided down toward the sublevel garage, a smug grin lingered on the handsome face. He certainly had quieted her, he mused with due appreciation for that unexpected fringe benefit of such a delightful experience. It had been worth the wait. Gillian Montgomery, artist, was a very passionate woman; it had been a long time since he'd been kissed with such feeling. If the stories he'd heard were any indication, she was truly her mother's daughter. No wonder Alex Strimling had risked all to cavort with the enemy!

As the elevator door opened, he walked quickly out. It had been lucky he'd had that pressing business to tend to; otherwise he might have been tempted to stay longer. But if a speedy departure was the only means of self-control he was to have in this woman's presence, he feared it might have to become a habit—until the time was right. Then, and only then, Gillian would be his.

CHAPTER 3

The patient on whom Mrs. McCoy went to check several minutes later was as a dark cloud hovering in a blue and gold sky. Surrounding her was sunlight, fresh air, landscaped verdure, yet she, at its center, brooded.

"Now, what is it, love? You look like you've lost a friend. Not so your Mr. Dawson. He was grinning like a Cheshire when he wizzed past the station just now. So what's the trouble?" Her plump figure bounced promptly into the chair that had been occupied by that very source of the problem.

Gillian regarded the woman with warmth, her appearance having broken the momentum of the sober contemplation that had begun to consume her. "Oh, nothing, really. I'm just having a time taking all this in, after seven weeks. Things are so different." An absent finger touched the small scar at the hollow of her throat, symbolic of her upheaval.

"You'll get used to them," the older woman said smiling. "We humans have an amazing knack of adapting to change. Don't worry, love. In time things will be right."

Her words echoed in Gillian's ears. Perhaps the cheery nurse had a point. In time things would be right. Never the same, though. Her parents were gone, bequeathing her an unexpected relative. Yes, she admitted reluctantly, all signs pointed in that direction. It appeared that she *did* have a grandmother. And she had Jed.

"Are you tired?"

"No, I'm fine." She *did* feel physically well, she realized with satisfaction.

"Would you like to go back to your room or stay here for a while?"

Gillian looked around, taking in once again the beautiful setting below her. "It's so lovely here. I think I'll stay for a bit longer."

A pudgy hand patted her arm. "Fine, love. I'll just run and take care of some paperwork, if that's all right with you."

"Of course, Mrs. McCoy. Go ahead. I'll be fine right here."

"You sure?" Gray eyebrows arched over her round face.

Gillian laughed softly. "Sure." Her blue-eyed gaze made a cursory sweep of the solarium before returning to the nurse's face. "After all, there's really no way I can get into trouble, is there?"

Chuckling in agreement, the woman stood to leave. "Okay, love. I'll be back to get you in a few minutes. Is there anything you'd like first? Juice? Coffee?" At Gillian's headshake, she turned with a final, "I'll be back."

She'd reached the door before Gillian's mind registered. "Oh, Mrs. McCoy?"

"Yes, love?"

"Could you possibly find me a pad of paper and a pencil?" Art had always been her salvation. Suddenly the urge was upon her.

"Of course! Be right there."

Within a few short moments, Gillian found herself sketching freely on the thick pad that the eager woman had produced. It was therapeutic, lifting her spirits enormously. Her subjects were varied—mostly segments of the wide panorama before her. She outlined the buildings of the university, the gardens and walkways. She reproduced the old live oak, whose luxuriant branches stretched up beyond her own perch, providing graded risers for the myriad of birds that serenaded so sweetly.

Her pencil set its own course, gliding evenly over the paper, leaving its trail of lead for posterity. As it covered

56

one page after the other, Gillian's mind wandered, taking her back to the happy times she'd known with her parents. For any faults they may have had—and it looked as though she'd been blind to at least one particular one—she'd loved them. Though she'd lived independently of them since graduation from college, she missed them now, knowing as she did that they were no longer a phone call away. It was a thought that filled her with a sense of utter loneliness.

Perhaps it was to combat that loneliness that she conjured up an image of the grandmother she'd never met. What did she look like? What would she be like? Why had *she* never contacted her granddaughter over the years? Why had her parents never said anything?

As on another occasion, she felt an unfathomable nagging in the recesses of her memory. *Had* her parents told her at some point in her life, perhaps when she'd been a small child and had subsequently forgotten? If so, why hadn't they reminded her—even better, introduced her to this grandmother—at some point over the years?

It had been her grandmother who had brought her so far from home. Why? Why, after all these years of denial, would the woman suddenly acknowledge Gillian? Or had it been primarily Jed's doing, this presumptuous transporting of her comatose person? He may have been, as he claimed, acting as a representative of her grandmother. What if, however, her grandmother had been no more willing a participant in this bizarre scheme than was Gillian? What if Jed had reasons of his own for taking control of her life in this way?

That was what rankled her. That was what, despite these dozens of questions that popped up at every mental turn, disturbed her most. Jed had, indeed, taken control over her. At the moment, he was in charge of her medical care, her wardrobe, her every physical accommodation. *He* was the only link between her grandmother and herself. Would *he* be deciding when she would finally get to meet this woman? Mrs. McCoy had been all too accurate when she'd said that it was Jeremy Dawson who pulled the strings. What else had he decided—and how would it affect her life?

In a fit of rebellion at the feeling of helplessness that she found so repugnant, Gillian slammed down the pad of paper and the pencil and sat upright on the chaise. Perhaps it was time she made an effort, token though it may be, of controlling her own destiny once more. Gingerly easing her legs to the floor, she took a breath, sighted a goal on the far side of the room, and steeled herself to stand, then walk on legs that had only that morning been reminded of their rightful purpose. Teeth clenched, she moved slowly, more smoothly than she'd expected, toward her destination, oblivious of the fine film of perspiration that gathered on her nose.

Mrs. McCoy returned a few moments later to find Gillian triumphantly resting on the vacant chair that had been her goal. Her patient's smile, aided by the pink flush that lit her cheeks, told her precisely what had transpired during her absence.

"You made it! Good for you, love! Now you *must* be tired. Am I right?" She was the mother duck gently chiding her duckling for having tried its wobbly legs beyond the nest. Gillian could only grin and nod. "*Now* I'll get that wheelchair!" The tilt of a gray eyebrow over the nurse's sharply pointed gaze kept Gillian in her seat, the warning sent and received without another word.

Later, entrenched once more in the room where a short nap had fully restored the strength lost during her exertion, Gillian picked up the pad of paper, turning page after page to examine what she'd so casually sketched earlier. The scenic pieces appealed to her for their artistic possibilities. The lines of the buildings, the sweep of the walkways, the juxtaposition of man-made and natural was material ripe for the silk-screen process. She would keep these sketches, she vowed, for a later date, when, back in Essex, she could apply them properly.

Her breath caught as she turned the next few pages. Without realizing it at the time, the pencil had mirrored the thoughts she'd had then. Before her lay a series of portraits, rough and sketchy, but recognizable nonetheless. There was one of each of her parents, poignantly preserved in her mind's eye, now converted to a concrete image. Their expressions were warm and gentle, as Gillian chose to remember them. The loneliness returned as she regarded these faces; quickly she turned to the next.

It stunned her. With unsteady hands she raised the page, studying it curiously. What she'd drawn was the face of her mother, slightly altered and much, much older. The jaw and cheekbones were similar, as were the eyes. It was, in addition to the age factor, the expression that set apart the two portraits. Whereas she'd sketched her mother so lovingly in the first, on this she'd created a sternness that disturbed her. Instinctively, she recalled the thoughts that had prompted this harsher face. It had been her grandmother on her mind at the time; this was a projection of her image of what that woman might look like. If it was loneliness that had driven her from the first two sheets, it was sadness that steered her from the third. If she had, in fact, found a grandmother on the heels of losing her parents, she would have hoped for a warmth to replace that which had been taken from her. Listlessly, she turned to the fourth and final drawing.

It was skeletal, more sketchy even than the others. There was the mere suggestion of a head, ears, eyes, nose and chin. There was a smile, smug and skewed, the ghost of a dimple with the hint of the devil. There was no mistaking its source.

As she replayed in her mind the visit she'd had with Jed that morning, she blushed then burned in turn. His kiss had been the most breathtaking she'd ever received. But then, hadn't she felt the electrical current that had flowed visually each and every time they'd seen each other at openings? Should she have expected anything different when finally his lips had touched hers? That she had reveled in his kiss was an indictment in and of itself; that she had, further, rejoiced in the awakening of her womanhood was a judgment passed. A wave of guilt washed over her, plunging her into a well of self-reproach. Despite the awesome attraction she felt toward Jed, she knew so little about him, his past or his present. And what had he in mind for the future? With all these unknowns, her participation in his lovemaking was doubly inexcusable. She'd been taught caution. She'd always practiced it—until now.

As she brooded, she found herself becoming increasingly enmeshed in a web of emotion woven intricately about Jeremy Dawson. She'd worked herself up to a state of misery when, late that afternoon, Peter Worthin stopped by.

"And how's the resident miracle doing?" He grinned boyishly as he approached the bed.

She made the effort to return his smile. "Wishing she weren't in residence, I'm afraid."

"What, restless already?" He was well used to the complaint, though he'd imagined her to be a more patient sort.

Gillian shrugged. "Not really restless. I feel . . . in a kind of limbo. There's not all that much wrong with me, now that I'm able to talk about it"—she smiled briefly at the touch of humor, then frowned—"and I'm anxious to get back to normal—as much as that will be possible. Once I return home and start working again, it will be easier to get over . . . everything." She was thinking primarily of the loss of her parents, though there were those two other people who had to be included in consideration. It was fear, short and simple, that motivated her now—fear of an unknown future involving those two particular people.

The only solace she seemed to find was in the thought of returning north, to the home she knew. "When will I be able to leave the hospital?"

The doctor was puzzled by her unease. "Actually, you can be discharged within a very few days. I'd like to run some tests, just to make sure that everything is back to normal. You should work out a little more with the therapist and be able to get around sufficiently on your own. That left arm may be stiff for a while; I'd like to see you establish a regimen of exercise for it. Otherwise, if everything checks out, you're free." He paused, studying her furrowed brow, her clouded eyes. "What is it, Gillian? You look worried."

Quickly, she glanced away. "It's not really a question of being . . . worried. After all, I have a home, a career, and friends in Essex. I have sufficient income from my printmaking to live comfortably," she reasoned aloud. "It's just that . . . well . . ." Her gaze shifted back to the doctor's in earnestness. "I have this . . . this gut feeling that things have somehow changed—that there are other elements controlling my life that I don't even know about!" Pleading eyes searched his for understanding and found it.

"What you feel is perfectly normal. You've undergone an ordeal, both physical and emotional," he began softly. "You've been in a period of total dependence, which you've now outgrown. There's only one solution to your problem, and that is time. It will take time for you to adjust completely." He eyed her thoughtfully. "You talk of unknown elements controlling your life. Can you elaborate?"

"This . . . grandmother of mine, for one thing." She was direct and to the point.

"Ah, yes, Jeremy explained that you'd known nothing about her existence."

"Do you?"

"By all means! I'd met her even before she came up here to visit when you first arrived. Don't forget—I'm an old friend of Jeremy's, and he and your grandmother are very close." At the look of skepticism that lingered on her face, he went on. "She does exist, Gillian, and she *is* a lovely woman."

She shook her head, then threw her arm across her forehead. "It's so strange, to suddenly discover a relative like that. It raises so many other questions."

"She will give you no cause to worry," he reassured her gently. "And I'm sure *she* has no designs on your life." As soon as the words were out, he regretted them, for his own mind was remarkably attuned to that of his patient.

"What about Jed?"

He knew it was coming. He'd set himself up for that one. "What *about* him, Gillian?"

Even sensing his mild discomfort, she had to pursue the matter. "I know absolutely nothing about him, Dr. Worthin. Nothing! I didn't even know he came from North Carolina until Mrs. McCoy spilled the beans. Does *he* have designs on my life?"

He smiled, buying time. "If we're going to discuss Jeremy, you'll have to call me Pete, as he does. We've been friends for years, and, as the saying goes, any friend of his . . ."

Her grimace quickly melted to an eyebrow raised in wry amusement. "You're evading the issue . . . Pete. Does your friend have designs on my life?"

Unfortunately, the doctor knew his friend well enough to believe that anything was possible. Yet he could answer her truthfully. "To be honest with you, we've never discussed it."

"What have you discussed?"

"Relating to you? Your medical care primarily. Your present situation. Little else. Jeremy is a very private person. There are many things I don't know about him, and we've been buddies for a long time."

She was more relaxed now, letting her arm fall easily onto her lap. "Tell me about him."

He hesitated, unsure as to whether it was his place. Jeremy *was* a very private person. He'd learned that early on, when the two had nearly come to blows because of Pete's natural instinct to dig deep into the psyche. There were certain matters—high among them his family and his love life—that Jeremy Dawson *never* discussed. Once Pete had accepted that, they had become fast friends.

Sensing his reluctance, she clarified her request. "Basic things, Pete. Nothing really personal or controversial. Little things like where he was born, his educational background, what he does for a living. Little things—hah!" She laughed aloud at the intended joke.

"You really know none of that? Why did I have the impression that the two of you knew each other long before this?" Jeremy had given it to him, he realized, recalling the gleam in his friend's eye when he'd made oblique reference to a "beautiful artist."

Gillian was able to clarify the situation mildly. "We have seen each other, on occasion. But we never got into any prolonged conversation such that I'd learn anything about him." How unfair it suddenly seemed that he'd been privy to so much of her life, while she had been totally deprived! No more! "Start with anything. Stick with matters of public knowledge, if you'd feel better. I know nothing. And he *is* the one who seems to have his fingerprints all over my case!"

The doctor chuckled at her plea and its closing analogy. The girl was sharp, without a doubt. In her subtle and refined way, she just might be a match for his friend! "You make a powerful argument, young woman," he sighed in resignation. Then, pulling up a chair and sitting down beside her, he volunteered what little he safely could.

"He was born and raised in the mountains of North Carolina, out by Weaverville. That's not far from the town of Black Mountain, where your grandmother lives."

She nodded; it was much as Jed had said himself. Remaining silent, she urged the doctor on with the sparkling interest in her azure eyes.

"I'm afraid I don't know much about his childhood or adolescence. He was sent to boarding school in Virginia, I believe. I met him for the first time during our freshman year at North Carolina State. We ran into each other in the dorm and in classes, became friends, then shared an apartment until graduation, when we went our separate ways."

"Obviously, you went to medical school," she interjected quietly. "What did he do?"

"He went on to get an M.B.A. at Wharton. Then he returned home."

"What does he do for a living?"

Pete smiled mischievously. "You could say he works the family business." Eyes dancing, he explained. "He *is* the business. His father was one of the founding partners, but it is Jeremy who has built it into what it is today."

Gillian's eyes widened in anticipation. "And what *is* it?"

"A multimillion-dollar corporation is what it is." There was neither resentment nor envy in his words, but rather a strong sense of pride in his friend's achievement. Gillian respected him all the more, realizing that he had knowingly chosen the less financially rewarding field of academic medicine but would have it no differently.

"Just what does this corporation do?" she asked softly, grateful for any information that might give insight into the character of the man.

"It was born in the tobacco fields. North Carolina is the country's leading tobacco producer, in case you didn't know."

Gillian raised an eyebrow. "I didn't know, but I'm sure it must bring in a bundle for the state, not to mention the specialists in pulmonary disease. Tell me," she chided gently, "are all of Jed's interests as dangerous?"

Undaunted by her sarcasm, Pete's grin broadened. "*You'll* give him a run for his money, I'm sure! But, no," he went on quickly, "the other interests are somewhat less controversial. The corporation is heavily involved in textiles, also a state specialty, and paper products. Come to think of it, the corporation has really infiltrated every major North Carolina industry." He paused, signaling an end to his monologue. "For any further details, you'll have to ask Jeremy."

"That's very impressive," she acknowledged softly, running quickly back over those Pete had given her. "What about his family? I know you said that he's a very private person, but you must know something. Is he married?"

There was obvious surprise in the doctor's expression. "No, he's not. But surely you knew *that.*"

Chestnut tresses slid over the pillow as Gillian shook her head. "I've always assumed it, but somehow too many of my assumptions lately seem to be proven wrong. He never mentioned a wife, though he never mentioned my grandmother, either," she added grudgingly. "So much has happened, it's getting so that I don't know what will pop up next!"

"The worst is over, Gillian. Take my word for it," he offered reassuringly.

A tired sigh followed his words. "Can I, Pete?"

He smiled. "Anytime. Please. I do mean it. And anytime you want to talk, just put in a buzz. Got that? Doctor's orders!" Her soft lips curved into a smile of gratitude, a smile more relaxed than he'd seen yet. It pleased him. "But any other questions you'll have to ask our friend, since I've got to be on my way."

There were other questions galore, which Gillian had

every intention of asking Jed, if she could only remain calm until he showed up. In the meanwhile, she would have to make do with that little bit of background Pete Worthin had just given her. Now, as the doctor stood to leave, she put a hand on his arm, her blue eyes reflecting sincerity.

"Thanks, Pete. I really appreciate what you've told me. I hope you weren't too uncomfortable talking about him."

"Well, well, it looks like the patient is bouncing back quickly." The deeply resonant voice from the doorway startled them both. Gillian looked up in time to see the topic of their discussion saunter boldly into the room, his dark face bearing a glint of humor sparked deep within by some other unfathomable emotion. He seemed, though she couldn't imagine why, annoyed. "She's a fast worker, Pete. You'd better watch out for that one." The glimmer of gold in his eye was sharp-edged. Gillian shuddered, remembering her hand on the doctor's arm only when Jed's gaze speared it. Quickly, she removed it, even then chiding herself for letting this demon rule her so thoroughly.

Pete was not in the least disturbed, but, rather, pleased by Jed's appearance. "It's the story of my life, Jeremy. Just when the going gets good, my bleeper sounds." He laughed good-naturedly, his clear innocence of any serious romantic notion toward Gillian relaxing his friend in turn. "I was just on my way, having only begun to answer this young woman's questions, most of which fall in *your* domain, buddy. So," he suggested, "I think you came at a good time. By the way," he added, glancing at his watch, "aren't you a little earlier than usual?" It was barely five o'clock; Jed wasn't usually in to visit before seven.

As had been the case for a majority of the past weeks, the patient here was a superfluous appendage. As she rested back against the bed watching them, the two men

66

launched into conversation, seemingly forgetful of the fact that she was no longer in a coma.

"I'm on my way to Atlanta," the rich baritone answered, "for a dinner meeting. Since I won't be back until late, I thought I'd stop by now. Seeing Gillian this morning made my day"—he paused to send a naughty glance toward the bed—"and I was hoping for as fine a send-off for the evening. I am *not* looking forward to this meeting." A slight grimace accompanied his words.

Had Gillian been included in the conversation, she would not have known what to say. From the initial pounding of her heart when Jed had appeared, to the puzzlement of his reaction to her hand on the doctor's arm, to the sheer fury of his remark and subsequent reminder of the morning's folly, to the sympathy she now felt at the fatigue that had slipped, in one brief sentence, through his otherwise composed mien—she was a bundle of confusion.

"Is Allan flying you over?" She flinched involuntarily at Pete's question; neither man noticed.

The black-haired one nodded. "He should be at the airport now, waiting for me."

"Then I'll get out of here"—Pete took the hint—"and leave you two alone for a few minutes. Have a safe trip, Jeremy. Gillian, I'll be in early tomorrow. Sleep well!" With a straight-armed wave in their direction from the door, the doctor was gone.

Gillian looked slowly back to find Jed's eyes studying her intently. All anger, if that was what it had indeed been, had vanished. Only the humor, flitting through those satanic gold flecks, remained.

"I meant what I said." He paused expectantly. Right on his wavelength, she took the bait.

"I'll bet you did! Unfortunately, I reacted quite differently." Her own annoyance could be denied no longer.

"Did you now?" The seductive drawl that assailed her

67

as he approached the bed threatened to belie her words. "Tell me, angel, how *did* you react?" So deep and low—he was a demon!

Desperately fighting his lure, she hugged herself protectively, absently rubbing her tender arm as she spoke. "You've got one hell of a nerve, you know, pulling something like that when I asked a very simple question that had absolutely nothing to do with it. You never even answered my question!"

"Hmmm, that's funny. I thought I had. Er . . . what . . . was the question again?" Mocking innocence coated the puzzled frown he gave her, as, before she could protest, he sat down on the edge of the bed. Having opened her mouth to speak, she clamped it shut tightly, her glower telling of her discomfort. Frantically, she attempted to ignore his nearness, ever disturbing, by barging on with her request.

"I would like to go home as soon as possible. I *asked*"—she emphasized the word in frustration—"if you could arrange it."

"I *did* answer your question, Jill." Then, very slowly, he asked his own. "Would you like a repeat?" There was no mistaking his outright amusement.

Knowing she'd been trapped, Gillian sighed. "Forget it. I wasn't planning to leave today, anyway."

"That's good. But *I* really do have to run." Successfully having put her off a little longer, Jed recalled his waiting pilot. "Tell me quickly, before I go, was it a pleasant day?"

Had he continued to mock her, she would have flown at him with renewed anger. His sincerity, however, curbed her temper. "Not bad. I walked, I ate, I've been poked around a little"—her pointed glance grouped him together with the medical staff—"and I even sketched."

"Oh?" A dark eyebrow arched in genuine interest. "Anything I can see?"

Instantly, she regretted having mentioned it. "No, ah,

not really. They were just . . . doodles." The last thing she wanted was to show him the sketch she'd made of him. It was far too complimentary, sketch that it was!

A knowing grin played on his well-formed mouth. "If I had the time, I'd argue with you. But as it is"—strong fingers lifted to curve around her neck, his thumb marking the scar at her throat—"my pilot is waiting."

The touch of his hand, so warm and soft and . . . intimate, sent an involuntary quiver through her. To her chagrin, she couldn't get herself to resist his grasp. Instead, she impulsively voiced the only thing that had come to mind. "Must you go by plane?"

He studied her for a long minute, the silence thick with unspoken thoughts. Yes, she was worried, though he couldn't accept that her fears were for him. No, he doubted her worries related to anything but the memories that haunted her. His voice was ever so soft when he answered, in a small attempt to lighten her mood.

"I did try happy thoughts and a sprinkling of fairy dust once, but I didn't get very far." The look of boyish bewilderment he donned for her benefit did the trick. She burst into a spontaneous giggle.

"That's terrific!" How he could have made her laugh, when she would have rather brained him, was a mystery. But then, wasn't *he*?

In the wake of her laughter, a different light entered his eye, soon to be reflected helplessly in hers. "So are you," he murmured huskily, moments before he bent to kiss her, much as he had done that morning, and with much the same response. His lips had no more than to tender-touch hers than she was set aglow. Instantly mindless, she fell under his spell, returning his kiss with the hint of passion ignited. When the hand at her neck moved down to her shoulder to caress, then head lower, she gasped. A long finger seared its steady path between the fullness of her breasts, a breath's touch that electrified her beyond imagi-

69

nation. She was still tingling from its shock when he lifted his head and showered her with a satisfied smile.

"That should help. Have a good night, angel. I'll catch you tomorrow."

"Jed—" she protested breathlessly, knowing not what she wanted to say but only that she did not want him to leave her.

He had risen and moved smoothly to the door, where, much as the doctor had done earlier, he saluted in casual wave. "Tomorrow!" Then the corridor swallowed him up.

He'd done it to her again! Astonished, Gillian raised a hand to her mouth. He'd done it again! What manner of power did he wield over her that his very nearness could drive every rational thought from her mind? What had happened to her since the accident? Where had good self-discipline gone?

Twisting about on the hard hospital mattress in a futile attempt to find a comfortable niche, astonishment heated, then boiled into anger. The audacity of the man! "That should help," he had said, as though she were a tidbit of sustenance to tide him over until the next meal. Exactly what *did* he have in mind for her? What were his feelings, his intentions? He was an agent of her supposed grandmother's, yet he toyed with her insolently. What was to happen next?

Of the many bewildered thoughts that ribboned freely through her mind, of only one thing was she certain: It was *her* intention to learn the answers to her questions—when Jeremy Dawson next showed his head!

Steadfastly, she stuck to that intention, mentally steeling herself for the confrontation. She waited the following morning. Nurses came and went, doctors came and went, therapists came and went, dieticians came and went, but there was no sign of Jeremy Dawson. Each movement at the door alerted her nerves in false alarm, leaving even greater irritation in its wake.

The afternoon was a continuation of the same, one moment of frustration leading into and augmenting the next. It was a welcome inspiration when, fondly eyeing the cards that had been sent over the weeks by friends and colleagues, she picked up the phone, dialed the operator, and placed a call to her dearest friend, the fellow artist with whom she shared the rambling old cottage in Essex. If memory stood her in good stead, her roommate would be busily painting in the attic loft they had converted, skylights and all, into a studio. The phone rang several times, then was answered. Her calculations had been correct.

"Marika, it's me, Jill!" she announced excitedly.

"Jill!" The shriek tore into her eardrum with delightful intensity. "*How are you,* Jill? We were so *worried* about you! It was like a rebirth when Jed called to say you'd come out of the coma. How are you feeling?"

The smile on Gillian's face would have been sufficient answer, had her friend been able to see it over the wire. So pleased was she to hear the familiar voice, a touchstone to reality, that she casually accepted the reference to her self-appointed guardian with barely a bristle.

"Great, Marika! It's good to hear your voice! Things have been so strange and new here. So much has happened." Her friend caught the sadness that had underscored the last words, remembering well the week Gillian had spent in the hospital in Vermont, her own discouraging visits to the bedside, and the intense loneliness she'd felt herself at the funeral of Gillian's parents. The pair had been well liked and respected; a multitude of friends and business associates had come to pay their respects. Gillian would have been pleased, she'd thought at the time, at how fondly her parents would be remembered. Marika, herself, had never fully understood that part of Gillian that had had to break away from home. But then, she'd never been Sarah and Tom's daughter.

71

"Are you up and about yet? Done any work?" Marika shared the compulsive drive that motivated Gillian when it came to art; it was one of the reasons the two had become fast friends in college.

"I'm getting there. My legs are still weak, but it gets better each day. And I have done a little sketching."

"Good girl! Listen," her friend went on with suddenly recalled urgency, "I sent along everything Jed asked for. Have you received the stuff?"

Gillian frowned. "Stuff?"

"Sure. Some of your clothes and things. Since you'll be staying down there for a while, he thought you'd be more comfortable, especially while you work, in your old things. I sent jeans and work smocks, underwear and all that, and one or two more dressy things. He said he'd pick up anything else you need down there! Wow, Jill," she babbled, running on at the mouth in excitement at hearing from her long-ill friend, "are you lucky to have him! He's really taken over and made arrangements for everything. And he's *so* good-looking!"

Much as she tried, Gillian could no longer ignore her friend's ravings and this new information that had been so innocently given her. "Looks aren't everything, Marika. You're right. He *has* taken over, but I wish like hell he hadn't!" Her annoyance was obvious.

"I don't understand you," her friend chided gently. "You were totally out of it. *Someone* had to take over. I remember seeing him several times at shows, but you never mentioned knowing him." What was she to have said, Gillian asked herself? Should she have announced that she'd fallen in love with a pair of gold-flecked brown eyes? An involuntary gasp accompanied the gist of her thoughts. Mercifully, Marika was too busy talking to notice. "I had no idea he was a friend of the family. You never mentioned a grandmother." So Jed had gone into the whole story, she thought resentfully.

Her voice was soft when she answered her friend. "I didn't know I *had* a grandmother until I woke up down here."

"Are you serious?" Gillian had to smile at her friend's spontaneity. She and Marika blended well; if only she'd had her by her side during the past few days, she might have fared better in getting the answers she needed.

After briefly explaining the situation, Gillian determinedly changed the subject, insisting that Marika fill her in on the local happenings. While half of her was revived by the gentle gossip, the other half became increasingly annoyed with each reference to Jed, seemingly entering the conversation unintentionally, yet a ubiquitous force nonetheless. From Marika's talk, it appeared that all of Gillian's professional obligations had been effectively put on an indefinite hold, that Jed had made it clear that she would be staying in North Carolina likewise indefinitely. When she finally hung up the phone, with a promise to call Marika back within the week, she was, if possible, more outraged than ever.

Dinner had been left untouched on the tray when, pencil in hand absently carving angry lines of thunder on her pad, her eyes were drawn by some inexplicable force toward the door. There he stood, black hair gleaming beneath the bright hall lights, dark suit heightening the mystery of his dark eyes and bronzed skin. Quietly and closely, he watched her.

Her lips thinned into a line of control, her hand clenched the pencil tightly, its lead tip digging mercilessly into the paper. She waited, gathering her wits, letting him make the first move while she plotted her own.

Silently he entered the room, his figure looming larger as he neared. It was as though he had sensed her agitated frame of mind. Caution bid him tread softly. When he stood beside her, his eyes traced a path from her own to the untouched tray and back.

73

"Wasn't the food any good? You were to have the best."

Tilting her head back with a suggestion of rebellion, she held her gaze steady, her voice even. "I wasn't hungry."

"You need to eat. How else will you be able to build up your strength?"

As though the power of his eyes holding hers weren't strong enough, the gentleness of his tone threatened to erode her resolve. Struggling already, she tore her gaze away, looking down to doodle on the pad. "I'll build it up."

A long silence preceded his next words. "Are you sure you're not hungry?"

"Yes." Eyes downcast, she willed herself to think of those all-important matters she wished to discuss with him. Her concentration was shattered, however, by one light blow.

"Do you mind if I eat, then? I'm famished!"

Her gaze flipped spontaneously to his face. It was a split second of dropped defense—and she was lost. There was a look of pure and boyish innocence on his features. A grin materialized, in spite of herself. "Help yourself," she whispered, then let the silence relax her as she watched him summarily down the substantial, by institutional standards, meal.

"I spoke with Marika this afternoon," she ventured softly, when he had removed the table and its now empty tray from its spot bridging the bed, allowing him access to a seat beside her. "She mentioned sending some things for me. She seems to have the mistaken notion that I'll be staying in North Carolina for a while." Her accusation was open.

His brown-eyed gaze grew darker than she'd ever seen it, gold shards having been momentarily swallowed by intensity. "You will be."

Her insides knotted. Despite their brevity, there was an utter finality to his words that dismayed her. How could she fight him? Slowly and silently, she shook her head. "No, Jed. I won't."

Ignoring her denial, he elaborated as though he hadn't even heard it. "I did receive the clothes Marika sent. She's a lovely girl, by the way. She's been a big help from that end."

"Why did you cancel all of my shows and other commitments?" She willed a dose of steel into her tone, but failed dismally to produced anything other than an undercurrent of confusion.

"Because"—he speared her again—"you will be staying down here for a while."

Again she shook her head. "No, Jed. I'm going home."

A faint smile flickered on his otherwise sober face. "That's right." It was all he said, yet instinctively Gillian knew they were playing with words.

She owed it to herself to try a final time to penetrate the bold veneer before her. "I'm going back to Essex as soon as I'm discharged."

Now he shook his head, sighing. "You're coming with me, Jill, tomorrow. You'll be staying at my place for a while. When you feel strong enough, you'll be meeting your grandmother. Then, and only then, will you make any decision about returning north."

"That's unfair! It's not your right—"

"It *is* most certainly my right, considering what you've been through."

"But—"

"No buts about it! It's already been decided."

Gillian's chestnut mane preceded her deeper into the pillows, her determination sagging violently. Already spent from the day's anticipatory irritation, she was suddenly drained of all desire to fight, only wishing to understand.

"Why, Jed? Why must I stay here?"

He was unrelenting in his own quiet determination, as

75

he stretched a long arm to rest his hand on the bed just beyond her far hip. His pose was poignantly symbolic of the cage she felt herself bound in.

"You owe it to your grandmother, for one thing."

Anger gave her a renewed shot of strength. "I own nothing to my grandmother. She wanted no part of *me* for all these years. I owe her nothing!"

"You're wrong, Jill. You owe her a little of the love she's been denied for so long, regardless of who was at fault. And, if for no other reason, you owe her thanks for the money she has so stubbornly insisted on sending your mother each year. That money was supposedly for you. Just where do you think the down payment for that house of yours in Essex came from?" Gillian's jaw dropped, appalled at this newest claim. But he hadn't finished his indignant tirade. "Your father may have done very well over the years, but he certainly hadn't stashed away that kind of money, given the economy as it is."

"It was my mother's own—" she began defensively, only to be interrupted.

"Now where would your mother have gotten that sum?"

"She . . . saved. Don't forget, she was a successful artist herself." Her blue eyes pleaded that he believe her, that it be the truth. In their field of vulnerability, he softened.

"That much money, angel? Think about it."

She felt trapped. She'd always taken her mother's word on the matter. At twenty-one, when she and Marika had bought the house as an investment, as well as a home, she had been, perhaps, naive.

Her voice was a faulty whisper. "If I didn't know of any grandmother, how could I have known of money she supposedly sent. If it *is* true, I honestly didn't know."

She had a point that he was quick to recognize. And an infuriating point it was, on top of the others. For her

76

mother to have used this money without giving it its proper credit was inexcusable!

"I do believe you *didn't* know," he conceded softly, a hand moving up in comforting caress of her shoulder. The near apprehension in her rounded eyes had begun to affect him. Yet he had to keep her here, if only for a while. She had to get to know the mountains well to make a fair decision. She appeared so lost now—it was up to him to convince her. Quietly but firmly, he went on, his gaze deepening.

"You *will* stay, though. If not for the sake of your grandmother, you'll stay for *my* sake."

Bewildered, she began to tremble. "*Your* sake?" A quirk of amusement breaching his somber mien, he nodded his head slowly, in mocking echo of her own headshake earlier.

"Why?" Her voice was barely audible. It seemed she had been drawn once again into his aura of sensuality, stuck in its hold as a bug on a cobweb.

"I haven't gone through all this trouble to get you down here close to your grandmother only to have you turn tail and run at the first opportunity."

His words snapped her out of the web magically. "Trouble? What *trouble*? I never *asked* you to do *anything*. If anyone has had to go through trouble here, it's *me* and the arrangements I've got to make to get myself back home! And there's no way you can keep me here if I choose to leave." She was frantic.

He was totally calm. "You won't."

"How can you be so sure?" she challenged rashly.

His voice was throaty in response, his eyes alight with flame. "Because of . . . this . . ."

CHAPTER 4

For the first time, she fought him. With every bit of strength he'd left her, she struggled to resist his plundering mouth. He let her fight, knowing well that she would quickly exhaust herself. Her perseverance surprised him. What he hadn't counted on was that thread of fear that was never far from passion. And determined as she was that she would not yield this time, her senses were clear, as was that fear a factor.

Her hands pushed against his broad, crisp-shirted chest as he slipped his arms behind her back to pull her closer. She twisted and squirmed in a bid to escape, her head a moving target to which his lips clung doggedly in firm possession.

"No, no! Jed, don't!" she pleaded, when he finally released her lips to mesmerize her with his soul-reaching gaze.

"You need me, angel," he murmured in a hoarse whisper, his breath fanning her cheek, as heady an intoxicant as the warmth of his body, now so very, very close. "And I need you."

That she hadn't expected. Spoken at the very moment that her quivering limbs lost their last remnants of energy, she was suddenly all-vulnerable to his lure. Though her head had now ceased its frantic motion, his hands lifted to frame her face, his velvet-smooth gaze caressing her every feature as he held it immobile mere inches from his own. A wealth of sensation engulfed her in anticipation of past delights reborn.

"Kiss me, Jill," he urged softly, his deep voice plummeting to her own depth in a throbbing ache of desire, its rebound parting her lips in sensuous invitation. This kiss was gentle, emotion laden, ecstasy bound. Strong hands caressed her back as her own more tremulous ones clung to his sinewed shoulders, fearful only that he would draw away again.

There was warmth and comfort in his embrace, pure pleasure in his kiss. At that moment, she would let him take her anywhere, as long as he was there. His kiss deepened and she followed, willingly and passionately, his hunger a stimulant for her own. Her appetite had barely peaked when he gently laid her back against the pillows, freeing his hands for new discovery.

Arousal now mixed with curiosity as she let him touch her, his lips tasting her eyes, her cheeks, her neck, while his fingers explored her curves. Circling the fullness of a rounded breast, his thumb skimmed its fast-rising button, then teased and caressed in turn until she gasped in delight. As though reminded of her lips once more, his tongue traced their softness until, driven to a height she'd never known, she let them respond in wordless plea for more.

When a manly roughened hand slid against her skin, beneath the fabric of her robe and gown, to touch a naked breast within, she made no move to resist, but arched her back instinctively toward the source of such heavenly joy. Her own hands crept over his well-muscled back, delighting in their exploration of his virile lines.

Slowly, his lips left hers and seared a path to the point his hands had discovered, his tongue taking up where his thumb left off, in sweet, sweet torture.

"Jed, my God!" It was an exclamation of wonder, breathlessly delivered from high atop a cloud she had never dreamed existed. It was, ironically, those very words of delight that brought Jed down off the same.

Moaning aloud, he lifted his head and drank in her passion-glazed flush before hauling her roughly into his embrace, this one fierce, close, and infinitely two sided. "I do need you, Jill. I'll sweep you up, carry you away, and lock you in an ivory tower, if you won't come with me willingly."

Even beyond the force of his embrace and the thunderous racing of her pulse, Gillian felt the sense of peace that had settled over her. It was the first she'd felt since she'd awoken from her coma—indeed, the first such thorough peace she could recall from the whole of her adult existence. Complementing that peace was the intuitive feeling that he did need her, though she couldn't totally understand why. Yet, as the cloud dispersed and she drifted slowly, slowly back to terra firma, the peace was threatened by nagging doubts, deep-seated fears.

"You could be my knight in shining armor," she whispered wistfully, "but you'd be the very source of danger." Apprehension glittered amid the blueness of her eyes in silent appeal for guidance.

His bronzed hand smoothed the hair from her temples, tenderly and soothingly. "I'd never hurt you, angel. You must know that."

Reality crept up all too quickly. "I don't know it, Jed. I barely know you."

"Then I'll tell you once more, and you'll have to accept my word," he murmured, enveloping her once again in his arms. His lips tickled her ear as he spoke. "I won't ever hurt you, Jill. Please trust me. I know what is best."

So did Gillian—or so she'd thought before she'd come into the clutches of Jeremy Dawson. Now she felt more bewildered than knowing, more questioning than determined, more fearful than confident. He sensed it, as he drew back to look at her again.

"Will you let me keep you in North Carolina?"

She faltered, overwhelmed. In a bid for respite from the intensity of his gaze, she dropped her long, silky lashes. He would have no part of it. Strong fingers took her chin to tilt her face up toward his.

"Look at me, Jill." There was quiet command in his tone; only when she complied did he go on. "Will you stay?" Pause. "Please?" Pause. "For me?" Pause. "For your grandmother?" Pause. He scrunched up his face in mocking painful plea, an obviously exaggerated yet totally endearing expression. "Just for a little while?"

As seemed to be his forte, he'd managed to fish her from the maelstrom. Slowly, a smile of surrender crept across her heated lips. "Just for a little while."

She was to rue the words as soon as he'd left and the reality of what she'd agreed to hit her. She had, in a lapse of rationality, committed herself to remaining in North Carolina—even worse, to staying with Jed. The implications were multifaceted and dangerous.

Step by step, she analyzed the factors involved. There was her work. By delaying her return to Massachusetts, she would further delay the resumption of her career. Certainly, she could sketch and perhaps even paint, but her own beloved silk-screen printing would necessarily fall prey to the lack of a workroom and the required equipment. True, Jed had already cleared the way, from the Essex end, for her to remain here, but from the very personal point of view, even forgoing all formal commitments, she would miss the work.

In a strange way, she realized, she felt torn. Yes, she would miss that work, yet there was potential for a wealth of inspiration in those mountains to which Jed had referred. His words floated back along the winding lane of memory: the rolling hills, the forested high country, the purple mist. It sounded enchanting, she had to admit. She'd never been this far south in the Appalachian chain; perhaps she would never have another chance.

Then there was the matter of her grandmother. Although Jed's claim rankled her with the thought of an obligation to a woman she'd never met, her own curiosity was great enough to overshadow it. Blood did flow thick, she acknowledged ruefully. If she did have a grandmother, she had to meet her. It was an emotional need that could not be denied, particularly in light of the grief that still held a subtle grip on her. Perhaps the woman would be as stern and unapproachable as had been Gillian's preliminary sketch. But perhaps, just perhaps, she was the lovely person Pete had described, the lonely person Jed had outlined. In that case, they might each have something to offer the other. And in the matter of the money Jed did have a point. She had always been one to avoid a debt; if she did owe one to this woman, she felt impelled to compensate.

Finally, there was the matter of Jed—by far the most complex of the three. Here, as with the other two, her feelings were mixed. She felt an unfathomable attraction to the man, and had from the start. He excited her in new and awesome ways. And he had offered her those brief moments of a peace that she had thought to be beyond her ken. Yet he also frightened her, and in this case fear dominated. He had the power of stripping her, with one skewed smile and the ghost of a dimple with the hint of the devil in it, of intent and prudence. He knew just how to penetrate her defense, just how to manipulate her. Hadn't he demonstrated that very talent, to her lingering mortification? Never before had she let a man touch her as freely as he had done; and she had savored his touch—until her senses had finally returned.

This was the crux of her dilemma. Here she was, headed in the morning for Jed's home, in his company and at his mercy. Was she strong enough, emotionally, to handle *herself*? Therein lay her greatest fear.

It was a fear that gnawed at her through much of the night, depriving her of the curative luxury of sleep. Awakened in the morning by Mrs. McCoy, she was barely closer to a solution. The only stop-gap measure she'd been able to devise was a wall of caution, buttressed by tension and reinforced with fear. She vowed to be ever watchful of Jeremy Dawson.

As for Mrs. McCoy, she chattered on at the usual breakneck speed, her excitement for her patient marred only by her expressed regret, heartfelt and acknowledged with an appreciatory hug, that she would be assigned a new case later that day.

Fond farewells had already been bid the hospital staff when Jed finally arrived, travel bag in hand, to get her. Against her will and above her resolve, she found her eyes drawn to his gray slacks and open-necked maroon shirt. It was the first time she'd ever seen him in anything other than a very proper suit, and she was properly impressed. He'd brought her some comfortable traveling clothes—a pair of beige slacks, a white cotton blouse, and her favorite tan Famolares—all from the trunk sent by her roommate. Though he noticed the sadness that flickered over her features at the sight of the new piece of luggage to replace that which had been destroyed in the plane crash, he made no mention of it. Pete had already prepared him for the emotional strain she would be under during the next few weeks. She had said it herself. In the hospital she was in a limbo, detached from both the joys and the pains of reality. Now, on the verge of discharge, she was headed for a sharp letdown, as the inescapable and irreversible consequences of that accident made themselves felt.

Gillian herself was unprepared for the vague sense of depression that began to build as she dressed, then packed in the bag the beautiful nightgowns and robes that Jed had bought her. It swelled within her as she suffered the hospital rules and a wheelchair ride to the front entrance, where, with properly warm embraces, she bade farewell to Mrs. McCoy and Pete Worthin, who had made a point to be on hand with a promise to be out to visit her at the first opportunity.

It was only when she was comfortably seated in Jed's

luxurious silver Mercedes that she could sort out her thoughts enough to realize the source of her depression. The limbo was no more. She was headed for a new life. And as much as Jed had promised that it would be "just for a little while," she had the uncanny conviction that she had but barely begun to see the changes that that tragic accident would prove to trigger. For the immediate present, her thoughts centered on her parents, who had not been as fortunate as she. As she gazed out the window at the passing of Durham, the Gothic architecture of the university and its Canterbury-style bell tower, the blocks of tobacco factories, their trucks busily delivering raw materials in exchange for the finished product, she was filled with that same pervasive loneliness she'd but sampled earlier. This time it was greater, more real. For the first time since the ordeal had begun, tears gathered slowly behind her lids, filling, then threatening to overflow as she bit her lip defensively.

"How're you doing, angel?" His preoccupation in negotiation of the workaday traffic had not been so much that he had missed this, her first real show of an emotion he'd expected long ago. She was so strong, an introvert, yet so very vulnerable! It would do her good to let it all out, though instinctively he knew she would fight it staunchly. "You okay?"

Ironically, the sound of his voice helped. It diverted her thoughts to the present company and its ensuing dilemma, temporarily easing the burden of sorrow with which she would eventually have to learn to live.

Silently she nodded, grateful that his eyes were necessarily trained on the street while she gathered her composure. As the tears receded, she turned her own attention to the route they had adopted.

"Pete said you lived near . . . Weaverville, was it?"

"I do have a home there."

"Is that where we are going?"

"No. I also have a place a little closer, just west of Miller's Creek. We'll be going there."

She was puzzled. "But I thought my grandmother's home was close to Weaverville."

"It is."

"Then why aren't we headed there?"

"It's too far for you to travel in one day, for starters." He had it all planned out to the smallest detail. "Secondly, my home in Miller's Creek has a swimming pool, which will be good for your therapy. I believe Pete told me that your arm could use some work. Is that right?" He grinned knowingly at her, not bothering to wait for a response. "And, finally, the Miller's Creek house has a ready means of transportation nearby. I have to be able to get to work, you know." An unspoken something told her that the "means of transportation" was an airplane, and the thought sent a shudder of distress through her.

"How far is it to Miller's Creek?"

"If we were to drive straight, it would take a little over three hours."

"Aren't we?"

"No. I thought we'd stop for lunch along the way. Sound okay?"

This time he did wait for her nod before lapsing into silence. Again she trained her own attention on the passing scenery. In its way, the silence was comforting. It was perfectly natural, as was the brief description he offered periodically of the terrain they covered.

"This is the Piedmont, the central section of the state. It is loaded with industry. We are approaching the city of Burlington, home of Burlington Industries." She nodded in recognition of the name. "Beyond Burlington is Greensboro, also a leading industrial city. I have several textile plants there myself, though it also has cigarette, machinery, and electronics plants."

Her curiosity now turned instinctively toward him. "Do you spend much time at your plants?"

He shook his head. "Not if I can help it. Of course, I have to make an appearance every so often, but I pay people good money to oversee the day-to-day workings. I'd rather spend my energies at the administrative level."

"And where do you do that?"

"Our central offices are in Durham. I keep an apartment there."

Of course, she mused. That explained his ready access to the medical center. "Three homes—not bad," she murmured. "Which is your favorite?"

He flashed her a quick grin. "The one we're headed for."

Suddenly a new thought popped to mind. "You *will* be staying while I am, won't you? Or are you going to abandon me out there in the mountains?" Somehow the words were all wrong, though she feared that hers was a legitimate worry. Fully expecting a lewd rejoinder, she was surprised when his jaw tensed and his expression sobered.

"You won't be abandoned," he growled grudgingly. In the wake of his tone, Gillian wondered if he was, indeed, pampering her purely for the sake of her grandmother, if he had already begun to find her company an obstacle to his freedom. As much as that possibility would alleviate her greatest fear, she felt an odd disappointment—one that joined her latent depression to render her more subdued than ever.

Looking away from the darkly noble profile, she was suddenly overcome with fatigue. Within minutes the steady hum of the car's motor had lulled her to sleep, and she awakened only when a warm and gentle hand shook her shoulder. The car had stopped.

"Come on, Jill. Lunchtime. Do you think you can eat?" They were parked before an elaborately rustic restaurant —charming in its own reconstructed way, she mused.

After a moment, she sent him a teasing smile. "I'll try. I may just need that strength you talked about!" Only after she'd spoken did she hear the double meaning in her words. That she was physically under par from the ordeal of the accident was a fact; that she would need every bit of her old strength and more for future combat with this towering figure beside her was nearly as certain.

The combination of good food, sweet wine, and her own healing need conspired to induce her to doze on and off during the remainder of the trip. Though her sleep was a powerful defense against the lure of Jed's solitary company, she had to accept that he had, through easy conversation and a minimum of pressure, put her at ease enough to permit her that sleep.

The steady westward trek took them past Winston-Salem and on to Wilkesboro, where she awakened. As the center of Miller's Creek blinked its way past, the scenery grew more and more exciting, enveloped as they now were by the hills and furrows of the Blue Ridge Mountains. Not even Jed's charming preview could have prepared her for the sight that met her eyes when, after turning off the highway and driving up a winding mountain road, the car pulled into the circular drive of his home.

He said nothing, but silenced the motor, then turned to observe Gillian's response. The look of unabashed pleasure, which, for a rare instant, softened her every feature, was just reward for his having brought her here rather than to his urban townhouse. But then, he reminded himself, there had been other, more potent reasons for bringing her here to this more secluded spot.

"You can get out now, if you'd like," he prodded her in a gently teasing manner, reminding her abruptly that they had reached their destination.

Parrying his poke with a self-conscious smile, she opened her door and climbed out of the car to better see the home that would be hers for the next "little while." It was a spacious chalet, contemporary in detail, nestled in trees and hugging the mountainside. Unfinished pine and glass dominated her view; a long balcony skirted the upper floors, overlooking this circular drive whose hub boasted the last of the mountain laurel, white-cupped and exquisite.

"What do you think?" The deep voice was close by her ear, the warmth of his body touching her back.

"It's magnificent, Jed!" she exclaimed helplessly, turning to cast a genuine smile his way. Only then did the view before the chalet catch her eye; she gasped aloud at its beauty. Here were the rolling hills and the forested high country of which he had spoken. Here were layer upon layer of piggybacked ridges, stretching toward the horizon as far as the eye could see. Here were a myriad of valley pockets, tucked tidily between each ridge, with promises of meadows, streams, and fields below. The color was evergreen, dark and blue, broken by intermittent stretches of gay yellow poplar and lingering fuchsia-tinted rhododendron, dotted by a world of wild flower life just waiting to be discovered.

Jed fully appreciated and understood her silence. His had been the same when he had first seen this spot. It was serenity they shared, something unique. If only she could pass the long-range test as well!

"Here, let me show you around," he urged softly, taking her hand to lead her toward the large-paneled French doors, which at that very moment opened. To Gillian's surprise, an older couple emerged from the house, the gentleman grasping the woman's hand much as Jed held hers, and approached them directly.

"Gillian, I'd like you to meet William and Alicia Walker," he said, introducing the couple. "They run the house for me. William, Alicia, this is Gillian Montgomery."

The pair, who had regarded her intently from the start, now burst into genial smiles. "Miss Gillian, it's so wonderful to meet you and see you looking so well," the woman began. A petite gray-haired woman in her early sixties, she took Gillian's hand in hers with a strength belying her size. Then her more rotund, bald-headed husband all but stole Gillian's hand in enthusiasm.

"Welcome to the homestead, Miss Gillian. It's sure good to have such a pretty face here. Course, my Alicia's is pretty 'nough, but yours is a sight younger and fresher for Mister Jed, here, than the two of ours! I remember your ma and pa; you're the image of your daddy, aren't you?"

It would have been impossible for Gillian to miss the bullet-quick progression of looks that shot among the three others at that moment: the reproach sent from Alicia to her husband, the embarrassment cast from her husband back, the apology offered in Jed's direction by them both. Assuming that their reaction stemmed from fear of upsetting her with reminder of her parents, Gillian struggled to pay it no heed. Later she would wonder at their comment, since she'd never looked in the least like her father. Now, however, she returned their greeting.

"Thank you both. I'm pleased to meet you. And if you are the ones responsible here, you certainly do a remarkable job. Everything looks beautiful." The couple beamed at once.

"You have yet to see the rest," her host informed her, taking her elbow. "William, there's a bag in the trunk. Alicia, perhaps Gillian would like a hot bath and a rest. It's been a long day for her. We'll be in in just a minute."

Effectively dismissed, the couple scurried off each to his prospective chore. Only then, as a strong hand guided her through the graded landscaping and around to the back of the house, did she question him.

"I didn't realize you'd have help here. They are a lovely couple."

"That they are. William and Alicia have worked for my

90

family, in one capacity or another, since I was a boy. That's another reason I brought you here. I know they'll keep a close eye on you." His mischievously raised brow spurred her on.

"And *you?*" she countered impulsively.

He sighed good-naturedly. "Yes, they do seem to have been thrust into the role of chaperon. But"—his voice deepened—"make no mistake about it. I can send them on any number of errands to keep them occupied, should I wish it."

Her blue eyes flashed sharply. "I'm sure you can!" Chaperons or no, she'd have to be forever on her guard.

It was to be infinitely harder than she'd hoped as bit by bit Jeremy Dawson managed to chip away at her hard-sought resistance to his charm. For one thing, his home was a pure delight, its every modern convenience built subtly into the country setting—heated pool, wooded groves, spacious vistas, and all.

The greatest delight, where the house was concerned, Gillian discovered the following morning. She had slept long and well, making up for lost sleep and then some. Rising early and hearing no other wakeful sound about, she followed an impulse to explore those areas that she'd not yet seen. Dutifully, Jed had showed her through the living and sleeping quarters, the latter in an L-shaped branch off of the former. There was, however, another branch whose showing he had deferred to her need for sleep, her pallor and heavy lids attesting to this latter. Now, however, she headed for this branch, feeling fresh and relatively strong.

Each of the three doors off the central hall was open. The first, on the right, led to a study—book-lined shelves, oak-top desk, sturdy leather sofa all included. Jed's mark was on every inch, from the understated dignity of the furniture to the subtly masculine charm of the decoration.

This was his study—there was no doubt about it. Torn between curiosity and guilt, she reluctantly opted to move on to the next door, the one on the left.

This room, to her puzzlement, was totally empty, devoid of furniture, decoration, and personality. The bright morning sun was lonely here, as was Gillian. Quickly she headed for the third room, the largest of the three, located at the end of the hall.

One footstep into this room brought her to an abrupt halt. Stunned, she looked around, slowly and with growing astonishment, from one end of the room to the other. Her breath caught as she noted the overall layout, professionally designed and built, the overhead skylights and huge windows, and piece after piece of equipment, made to order and begging for use. Reflexively, her fingers ached to feel the silk beneath them.

"Will it do?" She hadn't heard his approach on the soft carpeting of the hall. Excitedly she whirled toward the door.

"Will it do?" she shrieked. "It's fabulous! How did you ever—"

"Marika helped. And Durham has several stores that are remarkably well equipped. And the mountains are home to any number of highly skilled craftsmen just aching to help." The broad grin that lit his dark face in a skewed white crescent was evidence of his own satisfaction.

Gillian's pleasure was boundless. "I can't believe it! You've got everything here—worktables, frames, silk, backboards. You've even got my favorite lamp, not to mention the sun!" She looked about at the shelves lining the walls and laden with supplies. As she approached, she listed their contents incredulously. "Paint, turpentine, squeegees, spare jars, glue, maskoid"—she directed her gaze to another large, flat work surface—"paper cutter, straightedge, matte knives. Everything's here!"

"All that is missing is the skill to apply it. You have that, Jill. Do you think you can work here?" Sincerity gave his words an added depth, which promptly transferred itself to her own clear blue eyes.

"I know I can." She hesitated then, not sure quite how to express her gratitude. It had been a totally thoughtful gesture on his part, touching her more than she could say. He'd had no need to do this. But having decided to do it, he had done it right, down to every last detail, even to the long line of clothespins nailed to a low rafter in anticipation of holding progressively each of the prints she might make. "Thank you, Jed." It seemed inadequate, but it was all she could do.

He disagreed. A firm hand took her chin in a feather-soft touch and his lips touched hers as lightly. It was a sweet kiss, simple and innocent. Then it was over. And *that*—the mere sampling of something so delicious—was, indeed, inadequate!

It was, however, indicative of what she was to expect as the days passed. For Jed was an icon of propriety—ever courteous and undemanding. If his outward behavior was to be the guide, her fears were unfounded. Never once was she the recipient of anything more than a short, sweet kiss such as that one had been. Never once was her traitorous body given the slightest opportunity for treachery. But her mind was, and it became increasingly besieged by such thoughts, thrilling, then mortifying, her in turn. She was the villain here, so it seemed!

Then there was the issue of her grandmother. With each passing day, when no offer of a visit was forthcoming, she grew skeptical, wondering again what Jed had in mind, whether this grandmother was reluctant, whether there was a grandmother at all. Parrying these worries, she delved into the offerings of Jed's gracious home. Her days were filled with sun, warmth, relaxation, and printmaking. The mountaintop panorama that her studio surveyed was captured in a series of prints, each layering color upon color in masterful application. She immortalized the red berries of the mountain ash, the soaring fronds of pines and hemlocks, the bloodline of acorn to oak.

Her studio became her sanctuary, the one spot where she could remove herself from all else but her art. As the days passed into weeks, she found herself seeking its solace more and more, in an attempt to escape the somber thoughts that dominated her wakefulness even in spite of that sun, that warmth, and that relaxation. Particularly, when Jed was gone, she suffered.

Faithfully, he had stayed with her during those initial days of adjustment, walking quietly with her on the mountainside, sitting leisurely by the pool while she swam, chatting amiably with her at meals, curiously watching while she inaugurated her new equipment—even breathing silently as she sketched the acorn-bearing squirrel by the old stone wall. Finally, however, he had to return to the city.

It was actually a comfortable schedule he managed to arrange, whereby he spent the mid-week days of Tuesday through Thursday in the city while the remainder of his work was done from his office at the chalet. The latter, in particular, had never appealed to him before, preferring as he had the active, traveling life of the executive. Yet now he found the more sedentary arrangement strangely satisfying. Never before had he looked forward to coming home from work as he did now. Unfortunately, he was as well aware of the cause of this change in him as he was of Gillian's very tangible melancholy. That her art pleased her was obvious. That she had begun to relax and enjoy his company was likewise so. Yet he could not deny the sadness that seeped through her veneer of appreciation and comfort. Despite Pete Worthin's warning, he personally had hoped for a speedier recovery. She was deeply locked within herself; if only he could find the key!

They were headed for a confrontation. It was inevitable. Each suffered the same loneliness, the same frustration, the same driving need. For Gillian that frustration spawned anger, her desire only to deny both her frustration and its cause. For Jed, on the contrary, there was but the wish to yield, to finally know the thorough satisfaction her goodness promised. For Gillian there was confusion, fear, and unsureness, tempered only by the solace of the silk. For Jed there was a growing sense of disappointment that he could not penetrate the wall she'd built. His hands were tied. There seemed but one means of intimate communication with Gillian, and that was potentially more dangerous than all else. For once he'd possessed her totally, he doubted he could ever be without her again.

The situation finally peaked late one moonlit Thursday evening. Having been gone since Tuesday morning, Jed was delayed in his return from Durham. Against her better judgment, Gillian had worried. Though he was ever careful not to say so, she knew that he flew regularly back and forth to the city. Her reaction was involuntary; she was frightened. The past few days had been particularly lonely for her, and refusing to allow herself to pine for Jed, her thoughts had turned to the memory of her parents. Perched now atop the balcony railing, gazing out over the purple and silver ridges of the night mountains, she mourned them, silently, soulfully. She missed them and what they'd always given so unconditionally. Love was a precious thing, a panacea for the aches and sorrows of the world. Now she was without it.

In a mood of restlessness, she crossed the balcony, slipped through the house, and headed for the back hillside. Passing the pool, she took the narrow poplar path for several moments, finally settling down atop a large granite boulder. The mid-August air was warm and still, its silence broken only by the rustle of the dried leaves beneath a bounding squirrel or the soft whisper of the wind in the hardwoods above. It was a beautiful night, she mused—beautiful and sad. For she liked to be alone, yet loneliness was what she felt; the two were worlds apart. Where was Jed? He wasn't usually this late, and she desperately wanted to talk. There were questions that could be ignored no longer, and he was the only source of an answer for most of them.

Happy as one part of her felt in this idyllic setting, the other part was ravaged with longing. There were still those nagging doubts—the thought of her parents and the warning they'd given her. What was it her father had said in those last tragic moments? The inability to remember magnified her frustration, and she kicked at the craggy rock in anger.

"Gillian?" His voice was distant. "Jill?"

"I'm here, Jed!" she called, remaining atop her silvered stoop.

"Gillian! Where in the hell have you been? I've looked all over the place for you!" he fumed, entering the clearing moments later, a glowering giant on the rampage. His tie was askew and his hair ruffled, the moon catching its shafts in sparkled rays.

"I wanted to take a walk," she answered hesitantly, startled by his fury, which had effectively damped, for the moment, all pleasure at his return.

He came to tower over her. "At this hour?"

"Why not?"

"Because it's not safe, that's why not! You could have tripped and fallen or had a run-in with the mountain nightlife—God only knows what might have happened! And you didn't think to tell either William or Alicia that you were going out, did you?"

She was properly chastised. "They were sleeping."

"Well, they're not anymore. I woke them up to ask about you, and they're probably out looking now! I think we'd better go back." Unthinkingly, he grasped her arm

96

with the forceful vise of anger. It was the arm she'd broken; its lingering stiffness was jarred cruelly.

"Ahh!" she winced. Immediately, he realized what he'd done; instantly, his anger faded.

"God, Jill, I'm sorry! Did I hurt you?" Abruptly, there was concern where none had been moments before.

But his unwarranted anger had been the final blow in a day, an evening of emotional trial. Fighting the tears that had suddenly formed, not so much at the physical pain as at the psychological pain she suffered, she gingerly rubbed her arm and backed away a step.

"Yes! You did hurt me!" she railed, giving vent to her own pent-up tension. "And I can't believe you're really sorry, so don't say you are. You're a bully. You've bullied me—oh, yes, in your own sweet-talking way—from the start. You've given me stories of a grandmother I don't know. When am I going to meet her, anyway? Tell me that!"

Her voice was tremulous in its rage. Jed had never heard it like that, or seen her as upset as she was now. Perhaps it was good. Perhaps he had finally broken through that barricade of stoicism. Sliding a hand into a trousers pocket, he stood back and let himself be the sounding board she so badly needed.

"There's something very strange going on here," she continued bitterly. "You've got me holed up here like a . . . a . . . a prisoner."—it was the only word that came to mind, and it tore into him like a dagger—"telling me what to do and what not to do as though you owned me. How long will you keep me here? When can I go home? Where is this precious grandmother who seems in no great rush to meet me?" Yes, she was hurt, among all else. "Tell me, Jed!" she screamed a final time, before slumping back against the coldness of granite. Then, shaking her head, she murmured softly, "They tried to warn me . . . they tried . . ." Drained, she let her voice break off, its sound a memory midst the soft night symphony.

Her words had cut him to the quick. He hadn't realized she was that unhappy. Had he refused to see? "Angel," he began, only to be sharply cut off.

"Don't call me that! It won't solve anything!"

His body became suddenly taut. "Neither will your self-pity!"

She gasped aloud, knowing even then that he was right. "I'm going back," she whispered meekly. He was perceptive and uncomfortably blunt; once more, she withdrew into her shell.

He didn't try to stop her, grappling as he was with his own warring thoughts. Rather, he waited until he was sure she had reached the house, then walked slowly back, his footsteps falling silently on the vibrant carpet of moss.

CHAPTER 5

Gillian went straight to her room. He had been right. Although each one of her questions had been legitimate, the underlying emotion with which she had blurted them out was inappropriate.

Filled with self-reproach, she stretched out on her bed in the darkened room. It was a lovely room, even lit now only by the indirect light of the moon. She had so much to be grateful for—this home away from home, her studio —Jed. As much as she might wish it otherwise, he had stealthily become a major—no, *the* major, if she were to be truly honest—motivating force in her life. Whether at home or in the city, he was never far from her thoughts. Was this, then, the major source of her quandary? Exactly what role did Jed play in her life? Exactly what role would he have in her future? It was the one question she could not imagine asking, yet the one that could put the others in perspective.

Restlessly she shifted position, then stood and walked to the dresser, then on to the window, overlooking the back of the house with its richly wooded slopes and paths. The glistening of silver beams on the mirrored surface of the pool caught her eye. Impulsively, she dug her most comfortable maillot from the bottom dresser drawer, stripped, and drew the slick-fitting swimsuit on. Towel over shoulder, she made her way quietly to the pool.

Sleep swathed the rest of the house. The night lights in the foyer were lit, as always, but otherwise there was neither sight nor sound of life. Jed must have returned and gone to bed, she acknowledged with disturbingly mixed feelings. She had so wanted that opportunity to talk—but she had blown it!

In a burst of renewed frustration, she dove into the pool and swam from end to end, time and again, until her arm began to ache. It was cathartic, this vigorous physical exercise; pushing herself for an extra two laps, she finally rolled onto her back to float in the moonlight. It was the movement of water from the far end of the pool that jerked her up in alarm, her eyes riveting in the darkness, her outcry halted only by the last-minute recognition of the sleek, black-haired head approaching in a leisurely crawl.

"You frightened me!" she exclaimed, breathless both from her own physical exertion and from the shock of sudden company. He pulled up in the water close by her, treading as he spoke.

"I've been watching you. You must not have seen me. I was sitting over there"—he cocked his head to a far dark corner—"when you came down."

It occurred to Gillian that he'd never swum with her before, but had always watched from the side, lifeguard fashion, supervising her therapy. His dripping features, electrified by the moon's reflection on the water, were all masculine and appealing, his shoulders rippling with muscles she had often imagined. Suddenly she felt the spark of a deeper emotion, with a breathlessness all its own.

Jed felt it, too. Passing visually between them as of old, it moved slowly down, through each floating body, then up again, giving direction to hands and arms. "Angel," he whispered, as he reached out to touch her neck. This time she made no objection to the appellation, responding to it by returning his grasp and allowing him to tow her to more shallow water. When finally they could stand waist deep in the water, he tightened his embrace, drawing her flush against him. He moaned as she wrapped her arms tightly around his neck.

"I'm sorry, angel. I promised I'd never hurt you—"

"No, Jed. I'm sorry. You were right—"

Their lips met then in a mutual silencing, slanting hun-

100

grily over and across, seeking solace in sweet ecstasy. For Gillian it was a new world, the hair-roughened contours of his chest so sharp through the skin-thin maillot, the sinewed sweeps of bare back so vital beneath her tingling fingertips. She sighed in turn as his lips left hers to nuzzle the sensitive cord of her neck. Cushioned by the water and cradled by his arms, she could think of no more divine place to be. When he kissed her again, it was pure rapture, an intermingling of life's breath so heady as to cast aside the flimsy remains of rationality, the far-off inkling of fear.

With masterful persuasion, his hands caressed her arms, her back, and her hips. Hers mirrored the motion, reveling in his muscled torso as she palmed his shoulders, his back, and, just below the water line, the lean lines of his hips. Then she gasped and drew away, startled.

"Jed?"

"Shhh, angel. It's all right. I won't hurt you," he crooned, his eyes deep and compelling, his hands bringing her back against his firm and naked body. Even as the warning sounded in the recesses of her consciousness, she savored the haven of his steel-banded arms. For enigmatic as it seemed, it offered her the intangible something she craved. For whatever was the nature of the power he held over her, she needed him. She did!

Her conviction was uttered in the renewed ardor of her kiss, as she returned the play of his tongue with her own. This time, when her hands returned to a more timid exploration, he lifted his head to look down at her. Gold flecks held her hypnotically as his thumbs slid beneath the straps of her maillot, then eased them down and off her arms. Helpless to move, she drank in the passion of his hungry gaze as it fell to the fullness of her breasts, exposed to his view inch by inch as he drew her swimsuit down to her waist.

Arms outstretched, she clutched at his shoulders as his strong fingers explored the twin peaks, circling, climbing, then cresting in turn. Desire mounted to molten need—she had never been as aroused before.

"What are you doing to me?" she whispered in a breathy groan, her eyes shut, her head thrown back, her fingernails digging into the flesh at his waist.

When once again his arms imprisoned her, she cried aloud at the feel of his chest crushing her breasts. An iron hand curved behind her head, tilting it toward his face. She saw the raw desire in his eyes even before he spoke. "I want you, angel. Badly." The very pain in his hoarse voice was the same as that deep within her, the pulsing knot in her belly that sent flames through her bloodstream.

"I know," she whispered, agonized by her own want, suddenly frightening in its intensity. She had been unprepared for all this.

His tone was husky by her ear. "Let me make love to you, Jill." His fingers slid lower to her swimsuit, then within it, gliding against her wet skin to slip the suit lower and off. But his action was one new step too much for her.

"No. Please don't, Jed." Longing in her eyes was replaced by fear, the long-instilled caveat to the virgin. Yes, that she was, but he had no idea. He saw her fear, however, and stared at it for what seemed an eternity. Then he sighed. And moved away.

"Go sit by the side of the pool and wait for me," he growled. "And pull up that suit!" Stunned by his anger, she did as he'd ordered, toweling herself roughly in self-punishment. Then she sat and watched as he swam laps much as she had done earlier. And she understood. This was his catharsis, too. She'd set a harsh task for him, asking that he cool his heated passion. This was his helpmate of necessity.

It worked. After ten minutes of vigorous lap-swimming, he slowed, then swam to where she sat, standing up in the waist-high water. Intimidated both by the precariousness of his mood and the magnificence of his body, barely hidden from view now, she forced herself to offer a light note.

"You are an excellent swimmer. I didn't know. You never swam with me before." She was unaware that her eyes begged for forgiveness, but that they did. He saw, studied them, then allowed himself a half-smile.

"Do you now wonder why?" His tone, the lingering undercurrent of sensuality, was answer enough. As she looked away in embarrassment, he grabbed the towel from her hands, waded toward the shallow end of the pool, deftly drawing the towel into a sarong-style covering, then climbed out. The moon lit his dark-haired legs and arms as he stood over her, took her hand, and drew her to her feet. Her eyes caught and stuck on his chest, its muscled breadth rekindling barely banked fires.

"Jill," he chided knowingly. "I'm trying hard. I'd appreciate it if you would, too."

Her blush was hidden in the darkness, but she dropped her head defensively, wordlessly. As his hands settled on her shoulders, she was bidden to look up.

"We have to talk, but it's chilly here. Go on in and get dry. I'll be up to your room in five minutes."

The protest on her lips was stilled by his knowing reflex. "Don't worry. I'm too tired for that. But what I have to say should not wait until morning. Now move!"

She moved, quickly and directly, to her room, where she changed into the most conservative of the nightgowns and robes that he had bought her. Precisely five minutes later, he knocked on her door, entering to stand on the far side of the room from where she had nervously retreated. He wore a pair of snug-fitting jeans and stood barefoot and bare-chested, Adonis reborn. Gillian struggled to maintain her poise, a task that he simplified.

He wasted no time getting to the point. "I'll make this short since I am tired." He ran long fingers through his damp hair in an effective show of that fatigue, then he sighed. "I was delayed tonight because I was waiting for a call from Henry Powell. Does that name ring a bell?"

It did. "Isn't he . . . wasn't he my parents' attorney?"

"That's right." He saw her stiffen. "Look, Jill, I know this may be difficult for you, but it's got to be said. First off, as I'm sure you would have assumed, you have inherited your parents' entire estate." She really hadn't thought about it; the thought chilled her. "Secondly, I owe you an apology." His voice softened but a hair. "Your mother's estate contains a large sum of money—every penny your grandmother sent was untouched. Your father probably never even knew about the account. It had been handled privately with Powell."

Gillian wrapped her arms around herself and sank deeper into the chair. As relieved as she felt that his earlier claim was wrong, she felt shaken to the core by the subject matter.

"You've come into quite a bit of money, Jill."

"I don't want it." To acknowledge this inheritance was to acknowledge the finality of her parents' death. She was not yet ready. During the ensuing silence, Jed studied her intently, his expression unfathomable. Finally, he went on.

"We're going to visit your grandmother."

Her chestnut mane swung as her head shot up. "When?"

"Tomorrow." There was indeed a finality about *that*. Having waited so long to see this woman, she was oddly apprehensive. Again Jed studied her for long moments; then, rising, he approached the window beside her and stood, hands in pockets, staring at the dark evergreen curtain. His back was a smoothly muscled mass of bronze, a heady lure to her trembling hands. Helplessly, her gaze caressed what her hands could not. When he turned abruptly to face her, she looked quickly down.

His voice was soft. "One other thing. I want your word, Jill—your word—before you meet your grandmother, that you will stay here in North Carolina for six months more. I want you to be able to honestly tell her you'll be here for Thanksgiving and the holidays, at least until February. You can give her whatever excuse you feel best, but I want you to tell her you'll stay." He hesitated, giving her a chance to ingest his command. "Your word. Do I have it?"

Relief washed over her in torrents. If he thought she'd fight his dictate, he was mistaken. Even she was surprised. Yes, there was pleasure to finally know *something* about the future, rather than this day-to-day indecision she'd been living. And, yes, there was a hint of rebellion against his attitude of authority. But, she realized with a start, she really *did* want to stay. There was an enigmatic attachment she already felt for this man and his land, his home, his life. She *did* want to stay, yet she couldn't totally understand why. There was everything she'd had and known in Essex—but it was so far away, both physically and emotionally, from her now. It had been so long since she'd dwelt on the old existence there—only now did that thought hit her.

"Do I have your promise?" he prodded, deep and low.

What motivated her question, she was never to know. Yet it popped out on its own. "Why, Jed? Why should I stay for six months?"

His own ready response was indication that he'd already asked himself the same question. "It's only a fair period to get to know things here—Your grandmother, the countryside, the change of seasons as we know them. Now that you're feeling well, you should begin to see what the mountains have to offer."

"You mean," she began in a teasing murmur, "you'll be letting me out of the gilded cage?"

A muscle in his jaw tensed convulsively. "Say what you will, but I want your word. Now."

His anger puzzled and upset her. Driven by an inexplicable need to appease him, she gave him what he wanted without further ado, for it was what she wanted as well. "You have it."

"You'll stay for six months?"

"Yes." The reward of the smile she'd expected and wanted never came. Instead he moved silently to the door, only there turning to face her briefly.

"Get some sleep. We'll be leaving at eight." Then the door closed quietly behind him and she was alone.

The drive was a peaceful one. Where Gillian had expected an awkwardness born of the aborted scene the night before, she was relieved to find the silence companionable, much as it usually was between them. Gradually letting herself relax into the soft luxury of the car, her gaze was drawn to the landscape by which they sped. The early morning mist had just begun to rise, leaving its thin veil of lavender hovering in scallops along the blue-edged ridges of the mountains, fading off into the distance as in a dream.

"It's very beautiful," she murmured in a soft whisper, neither expecting nor requiring a response. So engrossed was she in the view that she missed the look Jed sent her, a look deep and enigmatic, yet bearing the faintest hint of pleasured satisfaction. He had wanted her to see and grow to love these hills as he did; it seemed that they were off to a good start.

The sleek silver Mercedes easily negotiated the twists and turns of the Blue Ridge Parkway beneath the practiced hand of its driver. Where Gillian might have tensed at the hairpin turns or the sheer drop of the rocky cliffs, she was fully confident in his care. Her artist's eye roamed the rolling bluegrass pastures, populated sparsely by small herds of grazing cows, dotted but occasionally with token structures of humanity. The beauty of the vista was a visual intoxicant, drugging her senses with the peace of the countryside.

As the miles passed beneath their whitewall tires, however, apprehension crept slowly into the recesses of her consciousness, then bit by bit moved forward to full awareness of the momentous meeting about to take place. Gillian's mind turned to her grandmother, wondering anew what she would find, when they finally arrived at the site of her mother's childhood.

As the car rounded a curve, a roadside stand came suddenly into view. Propped atop the smoothed stone pillars of a low wall and guarded only by a pair of spotted cows munching lazily in the bordering meadow were a gaily gathered assortment—long rows of jars with their varicolored homegrown offerings of fruits, berries, pickles, and nuts, and deftly woven baskets brimming with the wealth of the early harvest of ripe red tomatoes, golden yellow squash, and plum-sleeved sweet potatoes.

"Oh, stop—please stop for a minute," Gillian cried out on an impulse, pointing a finger toward the sun-capped lids of the local wares. When the car was brought to a halt just beyond the impromptu food stand, she realized her impulsiveness. "I . . . I, ah, I would like to bring something with me . . . but . . . I . . . I don't have any money," she stammered unsurely in answer to Jed's puzzled gaze. Strangely, this was the first time she'd thought of handling money since before the accident, having lived the sequestered life she had since her discharge from the hospital nearly a month ago. "I'm sorry—I should have thought of that sooner," she apologized in embarrassment.

"No problem. Let's go."

He was out of the car in an instant; she followed likewise. While she closely examined each of the possibilities, delighting in the charm of the colorful scene as well, he stood to the side, delighting on his own in the very charm of her, impressed by the gesture of thoughtfulness that had spurred the stop.

"They're all so beautiful," she exclaimed, raising one jar to peer at the translucence of sweet-soaking cucumbers through the slant of the morning sun. "How about this one?" She turned toward him. "It's so refreshing looking. Would she like it?"

Straightening from his casual slant against a broad maple, he took the jar from her hand. "Refreshing they do look, but it will be the smell, the taste, and the texture that matter to your grandmother. You've made a fine choice!" Reaching into a pocket, he drew out the proper amount of money, tucked it into the empty can left for the purpose, and escorted her back to the car. For a brief moment she turned to look at the scene a final time, thinking of Jed's words. It was as though he had given her some clue to a strange puzzle. Yet he'd left so much unsaid! Was her grandmother a creature of sensation also? Did she, too, appreciate the texture of the wrinkled tree bark, the smell of the sun-warmed grass, the taste of the honeyed sunshine itself? Perhaps her grandmother wouldn't be such a bad sort after all, she mused, sliding down into her seat as Jed slammed the door behind her.

"I have some papers at home," he began, when he'd regained his seat behind the steering wheel, "that you can sign to have money transferred to a bank account down here. Not that I have any objection to paying—"

"I'd rather pay myself!" It was a reflexive snap that she regretted immediately, ungracious as it sounded for everything he'd done for her.

A grim line thinned his lips. "I thought as much. You're very stubborn when it comes to your independence, aren't you?" A definite tension had returned, and it was the last thing she wanted—or needed.

"I'm sorry, Jed. I do appreciate everything you've done

for me." Her eyes were soft, blue, angelic, systematically melting his taut mien. "But I've always tried to be independent, and though the last weeks have been totally the reverse, I would like to have been able to pay for those cukes myself. You understand, don't you?"

He gave her a shot of his skewed smile, though the dimple and its devil were noticeably absent. "I'm trying, angel. I'm trying." As his gold flecks seared into her, her innards quivered with an excitement too close to that of the night past. Quickly she looked away, to watch the land as Jed started the car and they moved on.

They had been on the road for nearly two and a half hours when they finally left the Parkway to climb a side road, marginally paved and lined on either side by the split-rail fences that were a fixture of the neighborhood.

"This land belongs to Amalia. The house is coming up soon, on your right."

Sure enough, within minutes, an aged wood structure came into view, small but two storied, with additions built on either side of the main body and a low shed visible far in the rear. A broad veranda fronted the house, looking out on the dirt walk and gravel drive. With a clatter of rubber on gravel, the Mercedes ground to a halt.

"The house has been totally modernized within, as far as plumbing and electricity are concerned"—he read her mind—"but the outside, excepting the normal upkeep, is much as it was when your mother lived here. Come on—let's go see if she's around." Jed's offer was a relaxed one, thoroughly in contradiction to her own mood.

"You mean she doesn't know we're coming?"

He shook his dark head. "I thought it might be best if we surprised her. It will be an emotional enough situation, without her having to have worried beforehand—as you did." A black eyebrow arched knowingly, giving her a sense of comfort. Perhaps he did understand what she had been going through. "All set?" At her deep inhalation and imploring nod, he took her hand and led her to the front door. Without a knock, he drew open the screen and entered.

"Amalia? Amalia?" He waited for sound of a response, but there was none. "Amalia? It's Jed!" Still there was no answer. As he called again, leaving Gillian at the front door while he walked through the downstairs rooms, she had a chance to look around. The house was as close to a colonial reproduction as she'd seen—a living room on the right, a dining room on the left, a hall and kitchen straight ahead, a stairway leading up just off center. It was furnished with ancient charm—nothing new yet everything beaming of warmth, coziness, and the quality that only true pride in craftsmanship can convey. It was, in fact, not much different from some of the houses she'd known on the north shore of Massachusetts, yet there was a spirit of intimacy here that most of those others lacked.

"Gillian." Jed caught her attention as he returned from the kitchen with a slim, auburn-haired woman in tow. This was a woman no older than fifty. Her grandmother? Impossible. Sensing her confusion, he quickly made the introduction. The woman, meanwhile, stared at her much as William and Alicia had done when she'd first arrived at Miller's Creek—as though she was a ghost returned from the past. "Jill, this is Mary, your grandmother's companion, housekeeper, nurse, friend, what have you. Amalia is in the east meadow. We'll go get her. Why don't you go into the living room and make yourself comfortable." His deep voice resounded amid the dark wood beams of the house, the richness of both synonymous with quality. Gillian's nod of greeting and agreement was received quietly, as the two others left the house.

Entering the living room, she felt herself suddenly and mysteriously surrounded by the familiar, a sense of history surging through her veins. Her eye passed over the deep-cushioned armchair, the worn wood rocker, the ageless

110

loveseat. It skimmed the hardwood floor, the hand-braided area rug, the half-cord of logs, split and stacked beside the hearth. She saw the fireplace itself, brick and blackened by decades of flame. And then her eyes lifted to the mantelpiece above. And there they stayed, held in astonishment by what she saw.

The old oak mantel was a veritable family photo album, most of its pictures yellowed with age, many cracking beneath the same atmospheric foe. There were pictures of men, women, and children whom Gillian had never met, side by side with those whose faces bore a marked resemblance to her own. If she had needed proof that this woman was a rightful relative of hers, she had to go no further. Her mother—there were images of her mother as a young girl, clearly recognizable to Gillian, though in none did she exceed the age of twenty. A family portrait, in particular, captured her attention—parents and two children, one of which her mother. Closely, and with the trembling of emotion sounding heavily within her, she looked for the first time at an uncle, a grandfather, both long dead. Then she saw her grandmother and was helplessly moved to tears. The same age, approximately, in that picture as her own mother had been at the time of her death, the resemblance was sharp—and much as Gillian had imagined it. There was a sternness in all four faces, but one typical of photographs of that time when the camera was still a beast to be feared.

Brushing the moistness from the corner of her eye, she looked further, only to gasp anew. Here was a collection of photographs of herself—grade school pictures, snapshots, her high school and college graduation pictures. There was even the most recent—a publicity photo on a gallery brochure taken no more than six months before. Once again the tears of a long-suppressed need surfaced. Struggling to swallow away the tightness in her throat, she raised a fist to her lips. At that moment the sound of the front screen opening, then the echo of footsteps on the floor drew her around, her expression frozen in unknown agony. Jed stood, tall and proud, beneath the high entranceway; on his right, clinging firmly to his arm, was a small woman, petite as her own mother had been.

Gillian's gaze widened, her tear-filled eyes joined in silent communication with Jed for a brief, supportive moment, before she approached her grandmother. They met her halfway, Jed's deep baritone a near-whisper soft, breaking the silence. "Amalia, Gillian's right here."

The delicately tinkling voice was fast out upon his. "I can tell that very well, Jeremy Dawson," she scolded him good-naturedly, as she dropped his arm to reach for the two hands that her granddaughter simultaneously offered. Her instincts were sharp, her aim exact. Blurred as was Gillian's gaze, it did not for a moment leave the kindly eyes that looked beyond her. "Gillian," she murmured softly, "let me see you, child." One small, fragile-boned hand lifted to trace the outline of her granddaughter's face, to draw out the sculpted jaw and chin, the high cheekbones and finely bobbed nose, the large eyes and slim-arched brows, the silky thickness of shoulder-length tresses. Gillian was held in a paralysis of emotion, as a small sigh escaped the elderly woman's frail lips.

"You're as beautiful as they all said you were," she murmured joyfully, her aged fingers having painted the picture her sightless eyes could not. For in the ultimate jolt of the day, Gillian discovered that her grandmother was blind. A mantelful of pictures, none of which she could see—all of which must have been described again and again to eager ears by every visitor to this room! As Gillian's heart ached with the years of lost time, her grandmother's hand raised once more, this time, and again with perfect accuracy, to wipe the tears from her granddaughter's cheek.

"But you mustn't cry, Gillian. This is a day for celebration. The tears are all spent."

Jed had stepped back from the two and now looked deeply at Gillian, whose victory over those tears was dubious. But then, he mused regretfully, she *hadn't* spent them, had she? It had all been bottled up for so long.

Gillian, herself stunned, was practically unaware that her tears had escaped until the loving hands of her grandmother brushed them aside. Yes, they were, indeed, loving hands, their touch filled with years of a yearning Gillian could only imagine. And this knowledge brought a new wave of tears to her shimmering blue pools.

"Come, dear. Sit down with me. You do have a voice, don't you? I haven't waited all this time to talk to myself, now, have I?" There was the same gentle note of scolding she'd heard used moments earlier to Jed, yet this one had an added element of humor. Gillian burst into a shy grin, her eyes glistening brightly.

"Of course not," she said, smiling through her tears.

"That's better, my dear." The older woman patted her arm as she pulled her down next to her on the divan. "Now, you must tell me about what you've been doing. I've heard it from other mouths for far too long, haven't I, Jed?" It was as though he was her source of reassurance also. Looking around, Gillian saw that he'd taken a seat in the rocker, its steady creaking a kind of pacemaker for the emotion-driven hearts that raced in this otherwise serene room.

"That's right, Amalia. You'll find it all more interesting from Gillian herself, I'm sure. She's a remarkable young woman, your granddaughter." His cocoa gaze melted any lingering nervousness Gillian may have felt, though it did nothing to bolster her composure. A fine time he had picked to praise her, she mused, her own adrenalin spurting beneath his steady eye hold.

Yet her grandmother, it appeared, was the remarkable

113

one, putting her at ease with a sprinkling of a smile, asking her question after question about her artwork, her health, her happiness in Miller's Creek. Deftly, she avoided those topics that might have been more uncomfortable, sensing instinctively Gillian's more shaky emotional state. The girl had been through so much, after all, she reasoned, losing her parents in such a tragic way. But then, hadn't it been her own daughter?—and Jed had said . . .

"Gillian, dear, your mother never made *any* mention of me to you?" The question had escaped the older woman's lips unbidden, evidence of the strain that she, too, had been under for so long.

It was an abrupt reminder of everything Gillian had managed to push aside in the course of their present-directed conversation. Now the full weight of the situation thudded back upon her shoulders. Her blue eyes flickered first to Jed's curtained face, then to the pleading one of her grandmother. Her voice was barely audible, as she struggled to say the right thing. It suddenly meant very much to her not to hurt this woman who had been so obviously hurt, as her whole manner now attested, in the past.

"I honestly don't know. She may have . . . but I can't remember. There was something"—her voice began to falter—"in those last few moments before . . . before . . ."—she caught her breath in incontrollable gasps— "before . . . the explosion, but . . ." She paused, agonized afresh by all that had befallen her since that tragic moment. "I can't remember. I keep trying . . . but I . . ." The knot in her throat choked off all speech. The tears were back—the aching, the loneliness, the raw grief.

Her grandmother took her hand in an attempt at comfort, just as Jed stood and spoke. "I'd like to show Gillian around, if I may, Amalia. She'd enjoy the meadow and the waterfall. We'll be back shortly."

The white-haired woman nodded, she, too, emotion laden. Gillian made no protest when, without another word,

114

Jed took her arm in a gently supportive clasp and guided her out the front door and down the garden path to the open meadow, where the clean mountain air could clear her head and her heart. But before the healing could begin, there was the old pain to be released, once and for all. Whether it had been the photographs, this childhood home of her mother's, the grandmother whom she'd never known, so sweet and giving and, yes needy of love—Gillian was overcome. No longer would the tears be willed away.

Sinking down on the soft grass by the low stone wall of the meadow, she curled her arms against the stone and buried her head, yielding helplessly to the pent-up sobs that racked her slim body. She wept soundlessly, a faint cry escaping every now and then as proof of her torment. The stone was hard and cold, as was the grief within. When Jed's strong hands drew her up to sit on the wall he straddled, she only knew that the solace he offered was warm and soft, alive and caring—for whatever reason, it mattered not.

He enfolded her aching body in his arms, holding her shuddering form close, cushioning her face against the smoothness of his shirt. The heat of his man's body enveloped her, chipping away at the chill within, though totally innocent of the sensuality it had oozed the night past.

"Let it all come, angel. You've needed to cry. It's been too long." He crooned by her ear, words of comfort and support, as he hugged her soundly, offering her a peace as healing as that fresh mountain air.

"I'm sorry," she stammered, when finally the tears had slowed and she made to pull away. But he held her still, with one arm around her shoulder, while the other applied a handkerchief to her tear-ravaged cheeks and gently smoothed moist strands of chestnut from her sweat-dampened forehead.

"No, don't be sorry, Jill. You were owed that one. It's been a tough time for you. I said that you were remarkable, but I know you can't be superhuman. And to be human means to let it all out sometimes."

"But in front of my grandmother? She's hurting, too!" There were the last remnants of tears in the pale blue eyes that looked into his.

He took her face in his hands, admiring its beauty even amid its sorrow. "I'm glad you can see that. She needs you, Jill. Do you now understand why you have to get to know her, to let her get to know you?" Wordlessly, she nodded. Thoughts of leaving these mountains, her grandmother, and . . . and Jed were suddenly alien to her.

"I knew you would," he murmured, gathering her into a final bear hug. Then he bent his head to whisper by her ear, "Let's go see that waterfall. Amalia may begin to get suspicious." There was a suggestion of mischief in his tone that helped clear the last of the tears from her eyes.

When they did return to the house, a hot meal was awaiting them. Both grandmother and granddaughter had recovered from the height of emotion each had hit before, and the conversation was surprisingly easy and enjoyable. An immediate bond had sprung up between the two, and, though again they steered clear of family topics, they found any number of other subjects to discuss. Amalia—for so she instructed Gillian to call her, cognizant of how strange the title of grandmother would be on the other's tongue—was intelligent and witty, eager to have others paint pictures for her of a world she couldn't see. Gillian was all too happy to comply, verbalizing the thoughts of the artist as she spoke. Jed remained in the background, satisfied to have brought the two together, finally, and with such heart-warming success.

Late in the afternoon, at the moment of parting, when Gillian embraced the woman she now knew to be her sole surviving blood relation, there was genuine affection given

116

and received, a promise of future help and companionship for each to look forward to. Returning to the car, Gillian was quiet, taking in the day with an outlook of happiness for a future she'd once thought lost.

"You look tired, angel." His voice serenaded her, topping the pleasure of the day. "Why don't you try to rest on the way home?"

"Why didn't you tell me she was blind?" she asked, gently ignoring his suggestion in favor of her own spewing thoughts.

He shrugged, smoothly turning the wheel to negotiate a turn in hilly mountain terrain now lit by the orange glow of the low-slung sun. "It wasn't important."

"How long has she been blind? I mean, all those pictures—did my mother send them knowing she couldn't see them?"

"Amalia has been a diabetic for nearly twenty-five years. I doubt she ever wrote your mother about it . . . or about the fact, fifteen years ago, that she had lost her eyesight. She's that type of person. She's very independent—like someone else I know." The deeply musical note of accusation in his voice told her exactly who he meant. With too many other questions on her mind, however, she overlooked his reference.

"How *did* she get those pictures? It had to have been my mother, didn't it?" It was a question that had gnawed at her all day, a puzzlement.

"Yes."

"But why? Why would she send pictures regularly to someone she refused to recognize otherwise? Why would she want Amalia to know about me if she had no intention of having us meet?"

Even as he said the words, she thought them. "Perhaps she *did* intent for you to meet. We'll never know." In Gillian's mind the same familiarity arose, the sense of knowing something yet not being able to recall it. Frustrated, she skipped on to the next question.

"Shouldn't I be staying with her rather than with you? Wouldn't that have been more appropriate . . . considering . . . everything." Her blush defined that "everything" for him.

His features warred between a return of an enigmatic tension and a hint of humor. Mercifully, the latter won out. "Amalia has enough to handle without worrying about you. Mary is a big help, but my home is more appropriate for, ah, entertaining. There's your studio—Amalia's house is too small for something like that. And then, of course"—his eyes twinkled devilishly—"there's the swimming pool. It's been good for you."

Mortified by his unspoken meaning, she looked away. Flames lapped at the charted ridges of the far horizon in the sunset, much as the fire licked at her nerve ends in brilliant reminder of earlier passion. What was it she felt for Jed? She felt helplessly drawn to him; she wanted him, yes; in some ways—such as the comfort he'd offered this afternoon—she needed him. He fascinated and frustrated her in turn.

She'd been given the gift of family—her grandmother. She had a home in the mountains for the next six months. She had an unfathomable relationship with a dynamic and handsome man. And she had her work.

Slowly the germ of a plan formulated in her mind, as the car moved on past the purple hills and the charcoal green valleys, past the sleepy meadows and quiet cowsheds. It had potential, this plan of hers, potential and . . . excitement.

"You can use my car, if you'd like." His voice startled her. For a minute she wondered if she'd spoken her thoughts aloud, so uncannily appropriate were his words.

"Excuse me?"

"While I'm at work, feel free to use the car. You're

certainly well enough to drive." A fine line of tautness skittered through his offer. Why the tension? It was the same thread that she'd noticed before, though its cause continued to elude her.

Determinedly, she ignored it. "Thank you. I'd love to have a chance to do some sketching locally. Maybe I can even find a small market for my prints." The wheels had begun to turn with greater speed in her brain, though she was not yet ready to share her broader ideas. "But I don't know, Jed. The Mercedes? It's a little above my style . . ."

His voice was deep, stilling her objections with a myriad arguments rolled into one. "Lady, *nothing* is above *your* style!"

It was the perfect ending to a perfect day, a day that was to prove a turning point for Gillian. She'd set down roots, quietly and subconsciously. Now it remained for her to nourish them.

CHAPTER 6

Jed's offer could not have been more propitious. During the next few weeks she used the Mercedes more than she had ever planned. It began with short trips to local spots to draw, then developed into longer jaunts into nearby towns to scout the local crafts shops and markets. Between each of her trips, she worked feverishly in her studio, designing stencils, painting each in its turn on the stretched silk, then forcing the paint through the screen for another color added. As she finished each completed set of prints, several were sent automatically back to Marika in Essex as proof that she was, indeed, working in this mountain hideaway.

"There's been a noticeable improvement in your work," her friend suggested during a phone call following receipt of the latest group of prints. "Not that I didn't love your work before, but these new things are deeper . . . more thoughtful . . . more mature. They're superb, Jill!"

The breath she'd been subconsciously holding slipped through her lips in relief. "Do you really think so?" Marika's opinion meant much to her, representative as she was of the art community from which Gillian had come.

"No doubt about it! Something must be agreeing with you! Is it the air? The rest? Your grandmother? Or that gorgeous hunk of a man you're living with?"

Gillian gasped. "Marika! You make it sound like something it isn't! Jed and I have a perfectly innocent relationship . . ."

"Your choice or his?"

"For Pete's sake, he's simply doing a favor for my grandmother!"

The argument sounded good, yet it stirred up a mael-

121

strom of emotion within Gillian. For, from that first visit to her grandmother, there had been a subtle change in the relationship between her and Jed. Where before he had treated her as a patient on the mend, now he saw her as a viable individual spirit. Particularly once she had her own source of support and free use of a car for mobility, she saw herself in that same way. And she saw Jeremy Dawson more and more in the romantic light in which she'd viewed no other man before. They spent hours together on the weekends, breakfast, dinner, and evenings together—barring those days he spent in the city. Gillian grew to look forward to this time with him—savoring his company, delighting in his good looks, reveling in the attention he paid her. However, that attention stopped short of a repeat of the passionate scene they'd played out in the swimming pool that night . . . and, much as she fought it, she was sorry!

It was so difficult to be near him, day after day, night after night, knowing of his sleeping form but a short distance down the hall, without being able to satisfy this increasingly nagging ache deep in her feminine core. They lived the life of a married couple in so very many ways—but one. Did she love him? He had picked up the pieces and put her together. He had comforted her, cared for her, and cleared the way for her to find herself. Did she love him? He excited her, warmed her, pacified her, and stimulated her in a way no one had ever done. Did she love him? She needed him—if he were to disappear suddenly from her life there would be a void comparable to that left so recently by her parents' death. She wanted him—yes, in her wild imaginings, she wanted him as husband and lover as well as the friend he already was. But did she love him? She was suddenly Amalia's orphaned granddaughter and, as such, Jeremy Dawson had come to her aid. Love, it seemed, was irrelevant unless it was returned as well. And she was certain that Jed did not love her!

That much seemed obvious in his manner toward her. He was a formal southern Sir Galahad, chivalrous to the hilt, yet proper, respectful, and agonizingly controlled. Aside from the few notable lapses when his virility had become his temporary master, he hadn't touched her in any more serious way than that of two very close friends. Even his outward behavior frequently puzzled her. That he enjoyed her company, after all these days together— and hadn't he had the perfect opportunity, despite his arguments, to let her live with her grandmother when she'd suggested it?—was clear to her. Yet there ran through his mood that fine grain of tension, at worst bordering on anger, that was an enigma to her. She felt that he held back a part of him from her, and as much as they were honest in their communications with one another, as much as they seemed able to read each other's minds at times, on this score she could never ask him. After all, what right did she have? He had never professed any deep and abiding feeling for her.

It was the constant frustration of this physical and emotional dilemma that eroded, in turn, the well-being that had been restored to her by her grandmother, her work, and the mountains. She felt herself walking a tightrope, standing straight at last but terrified of falling, for the net below her had holes that she couldn't, for the life of her, seem to plug.

Unbeknown to her, Jed was on a similar line; strung from the past to the future, moving unsurely through the present. He recognized her need for independence, but in respecting it denied himself the assurance he needed to steady his own course. He saw her adjusting to life at his home, giving and receiving Amalia's love, thriving in her printmaking. But it had been his own ultimatum that she obeyed in staying here. She, too, he sensed, held something back in their otherwise warm and open relationship, yet he had not the right to delve. After all, he had urged her to stay for her grandmother's sake above all. Why hadn't he been more honest then?

By mid-September, Gillian's highest hopes became a reality. Having labored long and hard in her studio, slapping the squeegee top to bottom, layering the stencils one upon the other, applying one, perhaps two new colors a day to the sixty-some-odd prints in each group, she finally had a portfolio of local work of which she was proud. This in hand, she left early one Wednesday morning, when Jed was far away in Durham, to drive east to Greensboro for an appointment with the director of his main plant there, Dawson Textiles, Inc. Jed knew nothing of her meeting or her intent, and she had purposely planned it that way, merely introducing herself to the director as an artist from New England, letting her credentials speak for themselves. For she wanted desperately—if this work were to carry the satisfaction for her she'd hoped—to do it on her own, without the help of the president of the corporation —much as she always had in the past.

As though Jed's invisible stamp of approval had preceded her, she breezed through the interview, duly impressing John Regan with her prints, further impressing him with her proposal to develop a new and exclusive line of handprinted silk-screened sheets and towels to supplement the top-quality line that this plant boasted. She had done her research well, not only choosing the plant and director most favorable—thanks to her evasively thorough discussion with Jed—to a new idea, but selecting the idea whose time had come. When she returned late in the day to Miller's Creek, with an appointment two weeks hence to negotiate a contract with Dawson Textiles, Inc., there was a satisfaction she'd not known in a long, long time. That night, she slept soundly, the success of the day temporarily blotting out the fact that she missed Jed terribly.

It was a night's sleep that would have to stand her in

124

good stead, for the next few nights were practically sleepless. Jed returned Thursday evening and, in good pseudowifely fashion, as had become the habit, she met him at the airport, some thirty minutes from the chalet. Originally her excitement at having Jed back enabled her to set aside her aversion to things aviatory enough to maintain her composure at the small airport. As the weeks had passed, she learned to turn a deaf ear to the goings-on there, only looking forward to the moment when Jed would be in the car and home once more. He teased her gently about it, ever cautious of reviving painful memories, yet she stubbornly refused to pass the main gate, never once even seeing the craft that carried Jed so regularly in and out of the mountains.

On this particular Thursday her pleasure at seeing him was enhanced, feeling as she did that much more of a person than when he'd left two days before. His mood, however, took an abrupt turn for the worse the moment he sat behind the wheel to drive home.

"Did you visit Amalia while I was gone?" Even despite the tension in his tone, she drank in the sight of him, so tall and lean, lithe as a mountain lion, the outline of muscles beneath his shirt and trousers, the lingering scent of the tobacco factory fading slowly into the clear mountain air, the shadow of a beard hovering with rugged appeal on his tensed jaw.

Unconsciously, she plucked at the tendrils that had fallen about her neck from the loosely upswept twist of her chestnut waves. Jed's eyes were straight ahead as she answered him. "No, she went to Linville to visit her friends. Don't you remember—she told us that last weekend?"

He grunted in reluctant remembrance. "Where *did* you go, then?"

"When?"

"While I was away." A coiled anger had begun to build, chilling his voice.

"I . . . drove around some." Puzzled by his edge, she softened her own speech. "Is something wrong?"

" 'Driving around some' sure as hell doesn't put *that* many miles on the car." His hard gaze ricocheted off the odometer.

Where she would have simply explained, his imperious manner stilled her voice. She owed him no accounting of her time that she knew of. "I refilled the gas tank at my own expense, if that's—"

"That's not what's bothering me!" he barked darkly.

"Then what *is?*" It was difficult for her to keep her own composure when he acted so strangely. Did he begrudge her the use of the car, after he'd initiated the offer himself? "If you'd rather I not use the car, I can have my own shipped—"

"Forget it." He glowered at the road ahead.

But she couldn't forget it. She was too hurt by his anger to forget it. "Please tell me why you're annoyed, Jed."

"I'm not annoyed."

"Angry, then."

"I'm not angry." He was furious.

"That's a laugh!" she muttered under her breath. "You don't seem to be terribly thrilled to be back here, that's for sure. Maybe you'd be happier staying in the city." It was a fear she hadn't anticipated, yet immediately it was one more knife thrust and twisting within her.

Silence hung like a pall during the drive home. When they arrived at the chalet, he hauled his bag out of the trunk and disappeared into the house—still without a word. The tension was drawn out into evening; by bedtime Gillian was in utter misery. To have Jed as displeased with her was an agony she had to try to remedy.

Jumping off her bed, she threw on the jeans and loose workshirt she'd left out for the morning, stepped into open leather thongs, and returned to the living room, where she'd left Jed earlier. As she'd suspected, he hadn't moved, but rather sat solemnly, as he had for most of the evening, a stack of papers strewn haphazardly, but untouched, on his lap.

"Jed?"

His dark head came up in answer to her call.

"I . . . have to speak with you . . ." Courage was suddenly hard to come by.

"Go on."

Slowly, she walked to the opposite side of the room from where he sat. "It's very difficult for me. I just don't understand you sometimes." His silence attested to the fact that she was now totally on her own. "I'm sorry"— she let her chin drop, a shaky hand fingering her forehead as she struggled to express herself—"I just want to know what it is I've done that's angered you." Her tortured blue eyes implored his response. For long moments he returned her gaze, drilling his own distress even deeper into her.

"And what makes you think you have the power to anger me?" he began suddenly, a hardness, a bitterness piercing her. "What makes you think *any* woman has the power to anger me?"

Gillian's gaze froze as, stunned, she stared at the cold face across the room. This was a wholly new sentiment he voiced. What did he mean? And what did he expect her to say? He accepted her silence, in turn, as he slowly pushed his papers aside and stood to stalk toward her. A dangerous element iced his look, steadily adding to her unease. He stood before her now, tall and menacing, holding her gaze in its upward tilt. She was already shaky when she heard his crude drawl.

"Women nowadays tend to get carried away with their own power. They're still best at one thing, and one thing alone." The thorough raking he gave her body took his words that one step further.

Gillian's fear was abruptly surpassed by fury. Instinctively, she raised a hand to slap the face that had addressed

127

her so crudely, but her wrist was caught short by a steel grip that drew it behind her and up against her back. Wincing in pain, she was forced against his hard and unrelenting form.

"Is that what you're best at, angel?" He spat out the words with venom.

She couldn't come close to a response, but merely whimpered, "You're hurting me, Jed." Her plea fell on unsympathetic ears.

"And I'll hurt you more, if you're not careful." His breath touched her brow in its closeness. "Leave well enough alone, Gillian. Don't push it. I'm a man who usually gets what he wants."

She was visibly trembling beneath his gaze, her arm a dozen wicked shafts of pain. "Please, you're hurting me," she begged a final time, but it was the subsequent buckling of her knees that made her point. As she collapsed against him, he released her arm to hold her quaking body for a short moment before sweeping it up into his arms. Ignoring her feeble protest, he carried her out into the hall, up the stairs, and into her own bedroom, by which time her renewed strength enabled her to fight him in earnest.

"No! Let me go! You . . . you brute!" she cried, squirming furiously to escape the iron band of his arms. Rudely she was dropped onto her bed and had just begun to brace herself to ward him off afresh, when he turned and stalked to the door.

"Go to sleep, Jill," he said, seething, slamming the door in rage, leaving her alone to cry her heart out on the soft satin pillow. It was a long, long time before sleep finally came.

As fate would have it, he took off Friday morning on a business trip and was not due back until the following Monday. The unexpected respite from a renewal of his anger gave her little solace. Despite all that had happened during that unfortunate afternoon and evening, she was as

128

lonely as she'd ever been. Despite the time-consuming schedule of printmaking she'd set up for herself, she missed him. Despite the conviction that his behavior had been unexplained and unjustifiable, she ached at the knowledge that a rift had come between them. When he called to leave word Monday afternoon with William, not asking to speak with her as he'd so often done in the past, though she was more than available, that he'd be going directly to Durham and would not be back until Thursday, she was distraught.

Sheer misery impelled her to venture to drive the distance to her grandmother's on Tuesday morning, intent on spending the night in sympathetic company. Amalia knew immediately that something was wrong.

"It's Jed, isn't it, child?" she began quickly, seating Gillian beside her on the veranda swing.

Gillian's voice was soft in its sarcasm. "How could you ever guess?"

"Why, it's written all over your face, dear!" Gillian couldn't help but laugh gently with this woman, whose instincts were dagger sharp. Her small, bent fingers could indeed identify the slightest worry line or crease of tension on her granddaughter's face. And today there were plenty. "Can you tell me about it?"

Had it been her mother asking, ironically, Gillian might have balked. When it came to men, Sarah Montgomery's opinion had been staunch and hardened. But this was not her mother, but her grandmother, once removed from that person who had kept such close tabs on her for so long. The feelings spilled out—those few she could express rationally.

"There's so much I don't seem to understand . . . about Jed *and* about myself."

"There, there, now"—the older woman patted her hand comfortingly—"one thing at a time. Now, tell me what's so mysterious about Jeremy Dawson."

129

She gathered her thoughts carefully before she spoke. "He can be very wonderful and straightforward at times, while at others he can turn angry for no reason at all. He seems to want me at his home, then he begrudges my presence. He offers me free run of the house, the area, then he gets angry when I do spread my wings. What's with him, anyway?" Her tone had become increasingly distraught. Amalia gave her a moment to quiet herself before attempting an explanation.

"What do you know of Jed?" she asked gently, then nodded as Gillian outlined what little she did know. "Then you don't know anything about his family life?" Gillian shook her head, sensing that, at last, that situation was to be remedied. Her grandmother continued quietly.

"It's only since you are, shall we say, emotionally involved to some degree that I tell you this, mind you. Jed treasures his privacy. I wouldn't normally think to violate it, but in this case it might just help you both."

"I don't understand."

"Jed never married. He's thirty-eight and should have done so long ago. He's attractive and well established in life. I'm sure he's had many a lady friend, but he wants a wife. He wants children."

"Has *he* told you that?"

"He doesn't have to." The white head shook slowly. "I can see it as clearly as that pert nose on your face!" Again the endearing reference to a sense that eluded her even as she was expert at it. "Now I ask you," she went on in her tinkling tone, "why has he never married?"

"I don't know. Maybe . . . maybe he has just never found . . . the right woman."

"Precisely!" the elder exclaimed with a rap to the back of Gillian's hand, perfectly aimed. "But take it one step further. *Why* hasn't he found the right woman? Can you tell me that?"

Helplessly, she whispered her dilemma. "No."

"I don't know for certain either, child. But I can make some pretty good guesses. He's never quite forgiven his mother for having taken off the way she did, just taking his sister and disappearing with her, abandoning Jed and his daddy."

"Sister? He never mentioned a sister!"

"No, he wouldn't. She was thirteen at the time and went along willingly. Jed was only eight, but he was acutely aware that they'd had enough of the hill country, the two of them. Made it very clear. They headed for the big city, where they just disappeared."

"He hasn't seen them since?"

The white-haired head shook. "Not a once." Then she paused, frowning, looking away. "Sounds too familiar for comfort, doesn't it?"

Intuitively, Gillian understood. "Amalia, about that—"

"No, child. Not now. Another time. You need to know about Jed first. The other is over, done. Jed is here, now." She paused again, finding herself once more. "He distrusts women, Gillian—distrusts their motives, their desires. He needs someone desperately, but he won't open himself to the kind of hurt his father suffered. It broke his daddy's heart, it did, when she up and left. And poor Jed had to stand helplessly by and watch. That was when he and I grew close. He needed someone. So did I."

This time when the note of sadness reappeared unmistakeably in her grandmother's voice, Gillian leaned forward to embrace her. Words were unnecessary in the moment of mutual comfort. And despite her quandary, there was this element of happiness that she could be something to, do something for, her long-lost grandmother.

"Do you understand him any better now, child? His motives and his own fears? We all have them, you know."

"But why would he take all this out on me? I'm not his

131

mother or his sister. I'm nothing to him but your granddaughter."

"And that bothers you, doesn't it?"

In her blindness, she saw everything, Gillian realized with a sigh of defeat. "Yes, it bothers me," she whispered begrudgingly.

A slow smile spread across the delicately wrinkled cheeks. "That's good, child. That's good."

Gillian was to wonder whatever was so good about it, but her grandmother refused to discuss the matter further. She had other plans. Commandeering her granddaughter's arm, she led her on a walk to the upper meadow, her own remarkable energy urging Gillian to move steadily across the soft bluegrass.

As they walked, Amalia regaled her with tales of the mountains and its people—tales of medicine blending, quilt making, and hog slaughtering, or basket making, leather working, and a heritage of lilting melody and haunting refrain. Gillian listened, entranced, to every word, successfully diverting her attention from Jed to the land he loved so well. It was a poignant story of a culture strong yet struggling, a story of families decimated by the loss of their children to the lure of the city, a story of pride, thrift, honesty, and a supreme regard for equality.

There was hope in the picture painted by her words, hope in the rebirth of the Appalachian folk culture as a recognized art form, hope in the restoration of forests once ravaged by the logger's ax, lands once raped by a hoard of gold-thirsty prospectors, hope in the return to the land of her children, seeking a life more simple and free.

"Will you read to me, child?" Amalia asked, when dinner had been eaten and the night world of the meadows had awakened to serenade them with the chirp of the cricket and the coo of the owl. It was a distinctively well-worn volume that she felt for, removed from its shelf on the side of the room, and handed to Gillian. "Have you ever read him?"

It was *Look Homeward, Angel* that Gillian held in her hands. Thomas Wolfe had been required reading in high school, and though she hadn't read him since, she recalled having been deeply affected by his vivid imagery. "Mmmm," she affirmed thoughtfully, her mind conjuring up images of the uncomfortably hard wood desks, the awkwardly adolescent students, and the stern but dedicated face of her ninth-grade English teacher. It was, despite its rough edges, a charming glimpse of the past.

Eagerly, she read the passages that Amalia requested, losing track of time with the turning of each page, losing herself in visions of this land about her, written by the powerful pen of a native North Carolinian. "He was from Asheville—down the road a bit, you know," her grandmother explained, when finally Gillian's voice grew hoarse from reading. "It is these mountains of which he speaks. Have you seen Asheville yet, child?"

"Not yet."

"Jed will have to take you, then. It's Wolfe's Altamont; you'd appreciate it much more having read what you just did. Though I must admit that the folks in these parts were quite stirred up when the book first came out. I was a young girl then, of course. Quite a stir it caused!" She smiled, nodding her petite figure in distant remembrance.

"May I hold on to this for the evening, Amalia?" Gillian asked, when the older woman excused herself to retire. "I'd like to reread several parts. I can understand why you enjoy it so. He has a way with words, doesn't he?"

"That he does, child. Now good night. And if you need anything, you holler for Mary, do you hear?" As though on cue, the third woman appeared to help Amalia. She was like a fly on the wall, ever unobserved, yet all-hearing. Now she cast Gillian one of the studied stares that Gillian had come to expect, then she escorted her charge upstairs.

For long hours Gillian sat downstairs, reading, thinking, reading again. Thomas Wolfe had seen, felt, known. The "limitless meadows of sensation," he had called them —those heightened perceptual moments when one had only to confront a a solitary thing to have its entire sensual aura imprinted on the brain. As an artist, she more deeply understood his image. She, too, could bring back the full sphere of sight, sound, smell, feel, and taste—all from the recognition of one of that fivesome.

Her eye rose to the mantel, falling on the recent gallery brochure in which her picture was prominently fronted. Reflexively, the sight brought back the moment of that opening—the throngs of people, the low hum of conversation, the taste of cheese and wine, the smell of tobacco, faint and slightly mentholated. Abruptly, she caught her breath as Jed's face materialized before her, his dark eyes brooding yet electric, his black hair gleaming, his jaw firm, his arms crossed over his chest as he leaned against the gallery archway, looking at her, into her . . .

Shaking her head to dislodge the image, she slammed the book shut. So much for the meadows of sensation, she mused ruefully, returning the book to its allotted space on the shelf. But thoughts of Jed were not as easily shelved, and she brooded long into the night, before the gentle hush of the wind in the oaks finally lulled her to sleep.

"Where in the devil have you been all this time?" The force of his thunderous roar over the telephone line shook her. She'd arrived back at the chalet no more than fifteen minutes before, having remained for the day to visit with Amalia. Though the latter had urged her to spend the night, Gillian had suddenly been anxious to return to her own home, as she had secretly begun to think of it. Now, at this rude welcome, she wondered why. "I've been calling all afternoon!" he continued angrily.

"But I specifically told Alicia that I was going to Amalia's and would be back late," she explained, more meekly than she might have wished.

"But driving through the mountains at night is crazy, Gillian! What's the matter with you? Have you no common sense?" He was furious at her. Evidently time and absence had not made the heart grow fonder. It had been nearly a week since she'd seen him. "Are you still there? Is everything all right, Jill?"

Her disappointment at his rage was such that she was oblivious to the sudden suggestion of concern in his tone. Sighing, she answered him tersely. "Yes. Everything is just fine."

There was a long silence, then, "You're awfully quiet, angel. I would have thought you'd be calling me names." His mood had miraculously seesawed, further puzzling her. "Do you miss me?"

He'd never asked her that before. Later she would ponder the question, and the totally unexpected effect it had on her. But now, that effect took hold, arousing the anger born of her own simmering frustration. "I thought I did until I walked back in here and heard your voice. Now I doubt it. You know, it was very pleasant to be away from any reminder of your arrogance," she lied, a wealth of stored-up hurt bolstering her. If only she *had* been able to exorcise all thought of him from her troubled mind, she might have had more patience now. Bull-headed in her torment, she stormed on. "And I don't need someone keeping tabs on me. If you can drive through the mountains at night, so can I! And as far as your calling this afternoon, I have no intention of waiting around for a phone call from you. I seem to recall that you didn't want to speak to me last Monday—"

"*I* miss *you*," he cut in with singsong accusation, seemingly unperturbed by her railing. But she was not to be calmed so easily.

"Fat chance! If you missed me, you would have made a point to be home Monday, like you promised. You've been running all over the countryside for the better part of a week. Don't tell me you miss me. I'm sure you've got better things to do with your time! And I'm sure you have better people to spend your time with! Now, I'm tired and am going to bed. Good night, Jed!" With a bang, she hung up the telephone.

Only then did she realize, with mounting horror, what she'd done. She had acted the part of the nagging, jealous wife! What had come over her? What did this man do to her, even in his absence, to warp her powers of self-control? Yes, she was tired, having slept little the night before, having driven the long distance from Amalia's, to top it off. And, yes, she did go to bed, as she had so curtly informed Jed she would. Yet once again sleep eluded her.

Not so the myriad of questions swarming hither and yon in her brain, pausing periodically to sting her with a renewed pang of guilt, anger, fear, or confusion. All thought was jumbled, all solution elusive. When, at two o'clock in the morning, she finally climbed out of bed to take two of the sleeping pills Pete Worthin had prescribed, she caught sight of her face in the mirror—and couldn't help but stare.

It was her face, yet it was different. Her pale blue eyes were bluer, her cheeks bore a natural pink flush that the mountain-channeled sun had painted there, her lips were softer, fuller, her hair loose and free, swirling and cascading like the brook on the hillside. Much as her friend Marika had described her latest work, Gillian herself looked deeper, more thoughtful, and infinitely more mature than she had back in Essex, before any of this had happened.

What was the cause of the change? Was she that different now, that her own face should so startle her? No, there was something else. It was more than the plane crash, than her parents' death, than the discovery of Amalia. It was more than her relocation to the Blue Ridge Mountains of North Carolina. This something worked from the inside out, starting from her heart and inching through her every fiber. She was in love. No longer could she deny it. *She was in love.*

The acceptance of this state brought tears to her eyes and coursing over the hollows of her cheeks before she'd even reached her bed. A weeping which she thought left behind that afternoon, in Amalia's meadow, now seized her, convulsing her limbs as she buried her head in the pillow. It was a lonely feeling, she'd discovered, to love alone. It was more lonely than anything she'd ever, ever imagined—more lonely even than the tragic loss still so fresh in her mind. For Jed didn't love her, or any woman.

Could he love? Could he learn to love? Could she teach him to love? Or would she be destroyed in the process? It was this new dilemma that bridged the gap from tear-filled wakefulness to drugged slumber, a slumber filled with wild imaginings and soulful dreams.

She dreamed it was real, this house-playing she'd lived for the past weeks. She dreamed she was Jed's wife, that he loved her as she loved him. She dreamed of spending days of happiness in these hills, sketching and printing in the fulfillment of one need, of spending nights of ecstasy in Jed's arms, holding and being held in the fulfillment of another need. She dreamed of waiting, waiting for his return from long hours in the city, of being rewarded by the warmth of his embrace, the heaven of his touch.

And then he was there. It was all so real. Standing at her bedroom door, magnificent of build, arresting of character. He passed through the haze of the pale moonlight to her bed, kneeling down beside her in wonder, kissing the streaks that tears had struck across the rose of her cheeks and the wide oval of her eyes. He took her in his arms and held her, with the strength of passion long denied.

It was all so real, as she lifted her arms to return his embrace, thrilling to the feel of his firm man's body as it lay down beside her, reveling in the softness of her feminity as it yielded to his hungry touch.

As her dreams played on, she romped in meadows of pure delight, all fear, all inhibition cast to the ever-blowing wind of love that harbored her. The only reality was here, now, Jed's arms about her, on her, hers moving likewise in sensuous caress. Every nerve end responded to him, every inner cord threatened to explode under the mastery of his touch.

His breath, mingling with hers, was a heady wine, his lips against hers a potent aphrodisiac. He explored her body with a thoroughness that inflamed her, kindling a fire deep within, a nagging, gnawing, persistent ache in her loins that begged for release. When the barrier of clothes became a source of torture, she willingly shed them, watching his mirroring actions with rapturous fascination.

It was so real as they stood naked before one another, so real as he brought her body into the lines and contours of his own, as real when he eased her down onto the smoothness of the sheets. It was so real as his lips, his tongue worked their way over her body, so real as her hands raked the thickness of his hair. It was so real as he held his weight poised above her for a last, infinite moment of aching desire, before gently, tenderly lowering himself, probing the heart of her femininity, then slowly, magically fusing their bodies together.

It was so real, her pleasure-pain cry at the moment of union, so real, his heart's blood pulsing above and within her, so real, the flight of passion that carried her higher and higher. And when she cried out again, it was at a joy she'd never, ever imagined, the joy of receiving his warmth, his body, his seed in a moment of mind-shattering ecstasy.

For long moments after, the thrill remained until slowly, slowly her breathing steadied, her pulse eased its racing, the tingling of her body faded to a lovely memory. Then, she looked up into eyes that stared back from an unfathomable distance—and she knew.

It *had* been real. Awareness flooded back over her. The faintly lingering quiver in her insides localized into a sharp jolt. *She knew. It had been real,* all of it. Just as he was here, now, his sweat-slickened arms straddling her body, muscled shoulders, strong neck, darkened features hovering over her. And his eyes, their amber shafts searching, searching for something. She gasped at the sound of his voice, the final proof of reality, a deeply husky vehicle for his own thoughts, as he gazed on her owl-round eyes.

"I had no idea it would be your first time, Jill. Did I hurt you?" He raised strong fingers to gently brush the hair from her damp forehead as, stunned, she merely continued to stare at him, trying desperately to grasp what had taken place. "Are you all right, angel?" he whispered once more.

Silently, she nodded. How could she not be all right when the man she loved was with her, beside her? The man she loved—her lover. As the fact gradually sank into her consciousness, she began to tremble. With infinite gentleness he turned her on her side and drew her back against him.

"Shhh, shhh. It's all right, angel. Everything's going to be all right," he crooned by her ear.

Much as she wanted to believe him, she could not dispel the feeling of fear, of near terror, that lurked within. She had ignored warnings, she had betrayed a principle that had been deeply embedded in her. Yet in doing so she had experienced the most reverent sharing she'd ever known. Why had she not expected that? Why had she not been told of the beauty of lovemaking as well as its potential consequences? In this she herself felt betrayed, angry, then, in turn, guilt-ridden. The trembling increased in force as, wordlessly, she lay in Jed's arms.

It was the sound of his voice, once again, that gave her perspective, its harmony a source of comfort, its words a lullaby. He was here, with her now. That was all that mattered. Somehow she would find the answers to her questions, but that was for later. For now, she willed the very nearness of him to gradually relax her. When exhaustion finally overtook her, she raised a timid hand to touch his arm, rubbing the textured roughness of its manly hair in assurance that he *was* real. He was real, he was man, he was lover. On the wings of that awesome trilogy, she fell asleep.

CHAPTER 7

It was late when she awoke, the midmorning sun already pouring through the curtains into her room. She was alone. As she stretched leisurely and yawned, all seemed as it always had been. With one notable exception. Her jaw clamped shut midyawn, as she clutched the sheet to her chin. She was naked. Her nightclothes lay casually draped over the chair, where he must have tossed them when he'd left.

Then it all came back—the pills, the dream, the awakening. Was it dream or real? Where was the fine line drawn? But she knew. Her body told her. Slowly, fighting a resurgence of the trembling she also recalled, she showered and dressed, then made her way toward the kitchen in search of strong, black coffee. Mercifully, no one was about—not William, not Alicia, not . . . not him. The coffeemaker was full, though, so she helped herself to a steaming cup, then headed for the back patio. It was a peaceful spot—just the place to begin to understand what had happened.

Could it have all been a dream? There was no sign of Jed. He was supposed to have been in Durham. Perhaps she had been more affected by the sleeping pills than she'd thought. Perhaps, in a sweat, she had undressed and thrown her nightclothes onto the chair. Perhaps it had all been a dream—a highly erotic one, but pure fantasy. Perhaps it had been a dream powerful enough to take credit for the lingering sensitivity within her now. Perhaps . . .

He watched her from the window of his study for long moments. There was a look about her, a lost, vulnerable

141

look that he hadn't seen since she'd first awoken from her coma. He had hoped to erase it for good, yet now it was back. What had he done? If only he'd known. If only he'd realized that she had been a virgin . . . before he had lost control! She was the most sensual woman he'd ever met, in her own quiet way. And as a lover she had been exquisite! In hindsight, it thrilled him to know that he had been the first. He had no regrets for himself. But did she have regrets? What did she feel? What would she want now? What if she wished to leave? Perhaps that would be her solution, but he could not allow it. He needed her too badly.

Driven by sudden resolve, he walked quickly through the house, slowing his steps only when he reached the back door. Quietly, he slipped out, skirted the pool, and moved to where she sat, wrapped up in the world of her own thoughts.

"Jill?"

She looked up, startled, then cast her eyes down again as quickly, his appearance both unexpected and unbidden. She had so wanted it to have been a dream, enabling her to harmlessly glory in its beauty, while avoiding the consequences.

"We have to talk, Jill. May I join you?" His voice was velvet smooth and deep, coaxing her response. Yet she said no word, merely shrugged and signaled her acquiescence with the wave of a hand toward the chair adjacent to hers. He sat, neither drawing closer nor venturing to touch her. "I've given this a lot of thought," he began, thinking of the years, the many years when he'd watched her from afar and wondered what it would be like. "We're getting married."

"W-what?" All color drained from her face.

"We're getting married."

His proposal, if that was what it could be called, hit her like a bombshell. It was the last thing she'd expected, when he'd so handsomely materialized before her. God, he was handsome! If she had finally had to take a lover, pills and exhaustion notwithstanding, she couldn't have chosen a more prime sample of the male species. But it seemed that he did not intend to be lover alone. Prompted by her blank expression, he repeated his decree.

"We're getting married. As soon as the arrangements can be made." His face was hard, almost grim, set in determination. If he had wanted, really wanted to marry her, he would have been pleased and relaxed. But this?

"Why should we get married?" She knew why *she* should marry Jed, and it had nothing to do with last night's passion. She loved him, it was as simple—or complex—as that! But he—what was his reason?

His gaze speared her. "After last night, I would have thought that would be obvious."

"Nothing is obvious to me, Jed," *except my love for you,* she added silently, "especially that you should want to get married." There was always that distant hope that he did feel something extra for her; with baited breath, she awaited his answer. He was to have every one . . . but the right one.

"It would seem to be beneficial all the way around. We share the house, the countryside, many interests, and Amalia. We've been practically living as husband and wife for weeks now anyway." His words echoed her very own thoughts after that last telephone conversation.

"Why did you come back last night, Jed? I didn't expect you until tonight. And after the way I . . . hung up on you . . ."

A skewed smile crept up his right cheek, stopping just short of a dimple. "You're not the first person who's ever done that to me."

Her chestnut mane flipped from side to side with her headshake. "I sounded shrewish," she muttered softly, appalled anew at her behavior then.

143

"A shrew of a wife . . . why not make it official?"

"But I don't want to be a shrew of a wife!" All she wanted was to be *his* wife, loved and loving. Could he understand that? She just couldn't spell it out—the words stuck in her throat.

His smile faded, his eyes darkened in utter misunderstanding. "Look, I think it's best we were married—and soon. I'm going to make the arrangements." Pivoting on his heel, he began to retreat toward the house.

Gillian's sense of self-determination was suddenly offended. "And if I don't agree?"

"You will." His broad back faced her, his voice vibrating like fine steel through the still air.

Driven by sheer desperation, she persisted. "How can you know that, Jed? How can you be so sure?"

Only after a protracted silence did he turn to face her, then begin to retrace his steps. "You were a virgin, Jill. You'd never been with a man before. Do you have any idea how rare a twenty-seven-year-old virgin is in this day and age?" Her cheeks burned as she looked away. "No, if you'd remained . . . pure . . . all these years, with *your* looks and with sexual mores as they are, you must have had very strong reasons. I can only imagine them. But if I'm correct —I saw that bottle of pills on your bedstand—I'd suspect that you didn't quite plan on last night happening the way it did. *Am* I correct?"

Her downcast gaze took in the narrowness of his jean legs and the brown sheen of his loafers, no more than a few feet before her. "Jill, am I right?" His hard-edged tone demanded an answer.

"Yes. I . . . I was dreaming . . ." she began in a whisper, only to let her voice trail off in embarrassment, before catching herself. "But it won't happen again!"

"That's my very point." His fingers slid to comb through the hair by her ear with deliberate seduction. "It *will* happen again. It was no accident. Sleeping pills or no,

144

you wanted it to happen as much as I did. You were ready for me, Jill. It's *sure* to happen again." His thumb traced lazy circles about her earlobe and the sensitive hollow beneath it.

"No." Her denial was barely audible, as her headshake lacked conviction. Every rational impulse bade her move away from him, yet she was held spellbound, powerless.

Suddenly he was down on her level, hunkering before her, his face even with hers. Both strong hands now cradled her head, softly, gently raising it so that her eyes locked helplessly with his. "Yes, angel, it will happen. Again and again. You're a beautiful woman with a very passionate nature. Now that that passion has been unleashed once, it will crave more and more."

"No! That's not true!"

His face was inches from hers, his breath warm against her lips. Her every sense reeled from the sensual onslaught —the manly texture of his skin, the muskiness of his smell, the strength of his features, molding her to his will. She was entranced. Ghost kisses darted over her parted lips. He was the masterful seducer, tempting, teasing, his mouth never quite touching hers, until she was fraught with frustration.

"Kiss me, Jed," she whispered mindlessly, her senses alive with the flame of desire. It was not until that moment, when he drew back to look at her, that she saw her own hands, one buried in the thickness of his black hair, the other played across his chest, a thumb caressing the curled tufts of hair at the vee of his shirt. He'd made his point decisively.

"It *will* happen, angel. You want it to, and I want it to." The bridled passion so evident in his eyes attested to his words. With measured movements, he straightened. "I'll make the necessary plans."

Pulse racing, she was motivated by a final rebellious gesture. "And if I still won't agree?"

The tensing of his body was a visible thing. Eyes that a moment before blazed with desire now glazed icily. "Then your choice will be to waive all rights to the custody of our child. No, don't look so shocked, Jill. You must know the facts of life. It's entirely possible that you conceived a child last night. My child. And no child of mine is going to grow up without a traditional family. No child of mine is going to be called a bastard!"

The gist of his words exploded within her—more so even than his proposal moments earlier. There was a deep-seated venom that even Amalia's explanation had not prepared her for. She shuddered at the meaning of his threat; if she should have conceived in that one delirious night of rapture, he would take the child from her. And much as she loathed the idea of a marriage without love on both sides, she could not bear the thought of carrying Jed's child only to lose it.

"Can't . . . can't we wait a few weeks . . . just to see, one way or the other?" Then she'd be able to know if she was, indeed, pregnant.

Slowly and menacingly, he glared at her. "It will be this weekend or not at all."

They were married on Sunday. It was a short and private ceremony, performed by a local judge in the intimacy of Amalia's living room. For her part, the older woman could not have been happier. Hadn't she envisioned just this from the very first day she'd met Gillian? No, it went even further back than that; hadn't she hoped for just this when she'd sent Jed north each year to keep tabs on her granddaughter for her? The glowing reports he'd brought back time and again were fuel for the fire; finally it had caught flame and Amalia was thoroughly pleased.

Gillian's behavior was model, playing the role of the new bride with sufficiently frequent smiles to convince the world of her happiness. And she *was* happy, that part of

146

her that loved her new husband deeply. But there was another part that was frightened, confused, and unsure. There was a part that sent dark and mysterious messages, messages from the past, haunting yet nebulous. There was something, she knew, that she couldn't remember. If only her parents were here to explain.

Jed knew all of the anguish that had gone into her final acknowledgment of defeat. In truth, he felt guilty for having pressured her as he had. But he needed her, he wanted her. The thought of her leaving was anathema! She was his wife now; he could make her stay.

Amalia had planned a wedding luncheon to follow the ceremony and it was shortly after they'd finished eating that Jed and Gillian departed in the Mercedes for their honeymoon, a week-long stay in his Weaverville cabin.

"It's not as fancy as the chalet," he reminded her, as they began the short drive, "but I think you'll like it."

"I'm sure I will," she answered quietly, feeling strangely awkward now that they were abruptly on their own as man and wife. Her eye fell to the wide gold band that ringed her finger. It was heavy, as though weighted down by the many doubts that assailed her. For if Jed did not love her, what was to happen? And particularly if it turned out that she was not pregnant, could she keep her self-respect as his wife?

"Having second thoughts so soon?" The fine line of tension reappeared.

"I've had second thoughts from the start. But then, you knew that." She stared out the window, avoiding his side-long gaze.

"You could have backed out."

"I didn't."

"Why not? I keep asking myself that, Jill. Why didn't you just turn around and hightail it back to Essex?" He was baiting her, digging for something beyond her.

She willed her voice to remain steady, though her patience had begun to wear. "As I recall, Jed, you listed all the arguments very nicely the other day."

He grunted. "A very docile wife you'll make."

"Don't count on it." The least expected statement drew the rise. "You know, Jed, you may think you've got me over a barrel, but I still have all that's tucked inside. You may take full charge of the incidental trappings of our marriage—the homes, the car, the wedding, the honeymoon—but you can't manage me quite as thoroughly. I still have my own thoughts. And I still have my own career. I won't let you take those away from me!" As she lashed out in frustration, she realized that those two things were all she really did have left of that independence, that power of self-determination she'd always prized. What had she done? She'd signed her life away to a man who didn't love her, who had married her for no greater reason than convenience. She'd known that before she'd married him, yet she'd gone along with the farce. Why *hadn't* she just run away? It would have been easy to get lost in the crowd. But she had never really considered that course, for it would have meant losing Jed, the man she loved. Now the question was whether the very depth of her own love could hold her together? Or would that love, unrequited as it was, tear her further apart?

Spirits were low when bride and groom arrived at the honeymoon cabin, each submerged in his own murky pool of thought, neither able to share with the other his fears. High among Gillian's were the prospect of the wedding night fast approaching. Jed had not touched her since the night he'd returned early from Durham, though she'd seen, from time to time, the heat of desire in his gaze. This time there would be no sleeping pills, no dreams to cushion her from the reality of his passion. And there would be no putting him off. She was his wife now.

"Can you get the door, Jill?" Laden down with bags from the trunk, he cocked his head toward the cabin. The keys were tucked under his arm; as she reached for them, her hand brushed against his body, its warmth searing her fingers, her own susceptibility infuriating her. As though to deepen her discomfort, he taunted her. "I'd carry you over the threshold, but after all"—his voice lowered mockingly—"we've been living together too long for that."

Determined to ignore him, she stalked to the door, only then stopping to admire the cabin. It was rustic in a well-preserved sense, with walls of rough-hewn logs, tightly notched and fitted at the corners, a roof of oak shakes, a wide front porch, and a monster of a chimney. A single-storied structure, it was small and rambling. Jed anticipated her thoughts once again.

"That *is* the original house, but, like Amalia's, it has been thoroughly renovated. There was never any need for a second floor—my father and I didn't need much room and we sure as hell hated to clean." His attempt at humor, plugged into that recurrent note of bitterness, was a dismal failure. Gillian pushed the door open and went in, looking silently about as Jed passed through with the luggage.

It was indeed a compact place, the original house consisting of one large living room—with open hearth—and a bedroom. Later a separate kitchen and modern bath had been added, as well as a den, a more intimate spot than the open living room.

"Can you cook?" he asked idly.

"Can you?" Let him stew, she mused, then immediately regretted her testiness.

With a shrug, he disappeared into the bedroom, giving her a moment's respite. What was wrong with her, she asked herself? Why couldn't she be civil? This moodiness was not her way! She had agreed to marry Jed; now she'd just have to learn to gracefully live with that decision.

In an effort to do so, she gave her full attention to the cabin. It had a quaint kind of charm she could not quite

149

identify—a sense of history that permeated every eave, every nook. Yet the furnishings were all relatively new and definitely Jed, from the sprawling gray sofa with its over-sized cushions, to the contemporary macrame piece hanging above the hearth and the hand-carved walnut coffee and end tables.

No, the sense of history was an emotional factor, planted in the walls, etched into the rafters. Perhaps it was the knowledge that Jed had grown up in this home, much as her mother had grown up in Amalia's, that affected her. Almost against her better judgment, she liked this cabin—she felt at home here, as she felt in these very mountains. There was something eerie about that comfort, however, that only added to her uneasiness; way back, in the recesses of memory, she sensed that she was a mountain person, that she had been destined to build a life here. It would have been such a lovely thought, if only she understood its cause and meaning!

"I'm going to the village to get some groceries. Would you like to come?"

His dark suit had been replaced by the more casual uniform of the mountains—a pair of slim-fitting jeans and a plaid shirt. In her biased eye, he looked as devastating whether in a suit, in jeans, or . . . or without. In silent anger, she chastised herself for her thoughts, then looked down at her own outfit—the soft peach linen dress, its matching jacket draped over her arm.

"No. You go ahead. I'm not really dressed for it."

Had he wanted her along, she reasoned, he would have insisted on waiting while she changed. Evidently he preferred to be alone. With sinking heart, she watched him leave, his back straight, his hands strong and steady by his sides, his legs long and muscular, flexing through the denim of his jeans as he walked. Aching with the desire to run after him, she stifled the impulse and went in to change.

Both bags were in the bedroom, a room more old-fashioned in decor than the rest. The furniture was hand-carved, dark, and sturdy—a high dresser, nighttables on either side of the bed, two high-backed chairs straddling the window. It was the bed that drew her attention—double in size, more intimate than the king or queen size of more common contemporary usage. It must have been his parents' bed, she mused, so old yet rich. A spark coursed through her veins at the thought of spending this very night with Jed in this bed. With a blush, she turned to her suitcase.

The rattle of gravel and subsequent slam of the car door announced Jed's return an hour later. Gillian heard it from the back porch, where she'd found a perch for observation of the gently trickling stream that wandered through the back yard and off into the meadow. The bumps and clangs of groceries being stored in the kitchen did not budge her from her post, though her mind's eye followed his movements with reluctant fascination.

"Let's take a walk." His hand took hers firmly, leading her down the few steps and across the thick carpet of grass to the adjacent woodland. As idyllic as was the locale, it did nothing to ease the wariness she felt, and at the first opportunity she withdrew her hand from his burning grasp. His nearness was enough of a temptation; staunchly, she dug her hands into the pockets of her blue jeans. His bold form chose the path, her taut one followed. It was a gradual climb to their destination—a small clearing that overlooked the cabin and its surrounding land. There he stopped, turning to survey his property.

"Tired?" His deep tone broke the silence.

"A little." Gratefully, she accepted the excuse he had offered for her quickened breath, its true cause a far cry from the invigorating walk.

"Why don't you sit down?"

Purposely, she chose a solitary rock, then eased stiffly

down onto it. One quick backward glance was all he spared from his thoughtful perusal of the landscape below. The silence that they'd shared so meaningfully in the past was now the source of a steadily widening distance between them. Conversation remained cryptic.

"Is everything in order?" she asked, grasping at straws.

"Just as I left it."

Nervous fingers plucked the dried cap off an acorn. "How far off is the village?"

"Down the road about ten minutes."

"You were gone so long, I wondered—"

"I bumped into some old friends."

"Oh." Plucking now at the petal of a mountain trillium, she kept her eyes downcast. As awkward as she felt here, the intimacy of the cabin terrified her more.

Finally, he turned to study her huddled form. "Did you bring a sketch pad?"

"Always."

"Will you be able to find subjects here?" He had picked a topic to which she could, at last, relate.

"Oh, yes." Her blue eyes lit briefly. "It's lovely here. The trees, the flowers, the hills out there, the cabin—it will keep me busy for the week."

His jaw hardened. "Good." Again he studied her. "Does it bother you?"

She looked up in surprise. "What?"

"Your arm. Does it hurt? You were rubbing it."

Her waves bobbed gently as she shook her head. "Was I? I guess I do it subconsciously."

"So it is sore?"

"No!"

"I'd like Pete to have a look at it when we get back. Any headaches or anything else?"

"No! I'm fine!"

"You'd sure fool me! You're as taut as a wire!"

Gillian knew that her tautness had nothing to do with

152

the accident, from which she'd now completely recovered. In a whirling movement, Jed turned his back on her, stalked to the edge of the clearing, took several deep and exasperation-filled breaths, and raked his bronzed fingers through the thickness of the black hair that had fallen over his brow.

"Come on. Let's go back," he grumbled. The note of defeat in his voice took her off guard.

"I'm sorry, Jed. I didn't mean—"

"Forget it!" His anger wafted back over the shoulder of his fast-receding form. Hastily, she followed, pausing only when she reached the yard to allow him solitary entrance into the cabin. Time crept as she lingered, hesitant to go in, hesitant to stay out. Finally, the latter triumphed.

A fresh salad had already been layered in the large wooden bowl when she poked her head timidly through the screen door of the kitchen. "So you *can* cook?" she asked, unsure of his mood.

"Can you?" The last of the paper-thin slices of purple onion sailed onto the top of the leafy mound.

Relief brought a soft smile to her lips. "I've had to eat something to keep myself sustained over the last few years."

"That's not terribly encouraging, Jill. You're too thin." All relief was short-lived, erased by the quickly revived edge. Determinedly she ignored it.

"What can I do?"

"Wash those steaks. Set the table. Then see if you can dig out a corkscrew from one of those drawers."

It was a very simple task made monumental by the proximity of the tall figure near her. He seemed to be everywhere she turned, despite the generosity of the kitchen workspace. When they finally collided, head on, he turning from the sink, she pivoting from the broiler, it was inevitable. Only in that moment did she realize that he was as tense as she.

153

"Gillian . . ." There was warning in the dark brown eyes that speared her in unspoken accusation.

Driven by her own exasperation, she threw the oven mitts onto the counter and escaped to the living room, burying her head on the arm she threw atop the stone mantel of the hearth. The pounding of her heart muffled the sound of his footsteps as he approached. When his hand settled lightly on her shoulder, she flinched, drawing impetuously out of his reach.

"Jill, I'm not going to hurt you. I just want to talk," he began softly, calming her as he would a skittish kitten. "We can't continue like this. It's damned uncomfortable. This *is* supposed to be our wedding day." His gentleness, more than his words, had an effect. Seeing the faint relaxation of her fist, he continued. "Look, I know this isn't the ideal type of marriage, but I think we're both going to have to try a little harder to make a go of it. Do you hear me?" Without raising her head, she nodded. "Look at me, Jill." Desperately, she fought his command. "Please, look at me?" It was the question mark he'd chosen, etched indelibly in the air, that drew her head up, her eyes to his. Large palms cupped her shoulders, tentatively at first, then—when she made no move to bolt—with greater conviction, turning her to him.

"Do I frighten you?" The warmth of his voice penetrated the chill of her body, reverberating from one end of her to the other.

Awed by the tenderness of his gaze, she could only muster a whispered, "No, not you."

"Then what? You look trapped, as though you are readying yourself for doomsday. It won't be that bad, you know, if you're worried about tonight." Had she felt much pain, he wondered suddenly? "Last time was the worst—"

Embarrassed, she tensed, then twisted for flight, only to be more firmly held by his hands. "No, don't run. I'm

154

sorry, Jill, if I seem to choose the wrong words. I'm just trying to understand. You confound me."

"I confound myself," she confessed quietly.

"Then let's start with first things first. You are frightened. Of something. You have that look in your eye. If it's not of me, I want you to tell me what it is of."

A frown creased her brow as her gaze darted to the side. "I'm frightened of everything. This whole situation is unreal to me! I know that I've had time to digest it all, but it still sticks right here." Shaky fingers flattened over her throat. "I feel frightened of things I don't understand—and so much of this I don't!" Beseeching blue eyes glanced up at him. "How can I ask *you* to understand what I don't understand myself?"

He returned her gaze for infinite moments before drawing her against his body. When she strained away, he let his arms slip into place around her back, effectively preventing her escape. His breath stirred the hair over her ears. "Don't go anywhere, angel. Just take it easy. We'll work it out." Hadn't she heard similar words before? Yet, dubious as she was, she wanted to believe him. "I want you to remember that I have no intention of harming you. Despite what you may believe, I didn't marry you to subjugate you to my authority or to deprive you of your individuality."

"Why *did* you marry me?" The words had come unbidden, as she raised her head to look into his face, so close, so dear. If only he'd say it . . .

A tawny finger ran along her hairline, tracing the now fading pink scar. "I've already given you the reasons. And they're not what's important right now. What's important is that we're on our honeymoon. It's a vacation we both deserve. You've been working too hard at home." At the surprised glance she shot him, he stilled her potential denial. "Don't give me that look." Beneath the spell of his gold-flecked twinkle, she was helpless to prevent the guilty grin from spreading slowly across her lips. "That's better," he crooned, again by her ear, as he hugged her soundly. This was one of the very things she loved about him—his ability to coax her into a smile when she'd thought they were long gone. Oh, yes, she loved him!

"Now," he began, clearing his throat dramatically, "let's begin all over again and take it slowly. You are my wife, and I want the best for you. We will relax this week, do some sight-seeing—do whatever we please. I won't rush you, Jill, *on anything.*" His meaning was clear, though the arched brow that framed his brown eyes promised clarification. "I'll even sleep in the den, so you won't feel pressured." Yes, she mused, that would certainly remove one source of pressure, though it might definitely aggravate another. But, as he had said, they'd take it slowly. And she did feel better about that.

Her sculpted features tilted more pertly up at him. "One other matter . . ."

"Ye-e-e-s . . . ?" He drew out his good-natured growl.

"I think the steaks are burning . . ." she whispered, then stifled a spontaneous smile in deference to the abrupt cloud of boyish dismay that seized his rugged features.

The steaks were viewed as a burnt offering to the forces of peace, which did prevail over the two of them for the length of their stay in the cabin. Setting aside all other worries, Gillian concentrated on enjoying herself for the week. And, miraculously, Jed's mood mirrored her own, making for a time of pleasure and relaxation. True to his word, he slept in the den, accepting that fate with a good sportsmanship that both astonished and puzzled her. It was as though, despite his having so graphically given their sexual attraction as a prime reason for marrying, he now no longer felt urgency on that score. Not so Gillian. For if there was indeed a lingering source of conflict, it was on this very score. It was, however, a conflict entirely within herself, an age-old one between denial and desire.

As the days passed and she ached to be closer to him than his maddeningly toying hand-holding, arm across the shoulder, or kiss on the cheek would allow, she realized that he had been right. With no amount of strength could she ever remain indifferent to this man and his virility. It was raw, it was potent, it was beckoning.

Mercifully, Jed kept her busy, intent as he was on fully acquainting her with the surrounding countryside. One day they spent driving through the mountains to the home of a potter, an elderly man whose primitive techniques produced a distinctive collection of bowls and vases to be sold at the local markets, one of which they later visited.

"It is a pity," she commented, after examining the potter's wares on public sale, "that he asks so little for his work. He could be earning a small fortune. These are magnificent!"

Patiently, Jed explained. "That's the nature of the mountain folk. They see their skills as a source of pride, their heritage, to be passed on from generation to generation. Sure, they have to support themselves on what they earn, but I often suspect that they'd be happier keeping their work to themselves."

Touched by the compassion he'd shown for these people, Gillian considered his point. "It just seems a shame that old Jonathan, for one, doesn't get his rightly due."

"You're an artist, so let me ask you." He ushered her through the door of a coffee shop and toward an empty booth. "Two coffees"—he interrupted his thought to call the order to the waitress behind the counter—"and two danishes, one cheese, and one"—he eyed her speculatively—"raspberry."

Gillian grinned. "How did you know I like raspberry?"

His smile skewed up into a whopper of a dimple, feeding her hunger in more ways than one. "Just guessed. Despite the little bits of grit here and there, you can be very sweet. Now where was I?" He parried the light kick to his shin with a nod to the waitress as their coffee was served. "As an artist, do you feel you are paid adequately for your work?"

"That's an unfair question, Jed. That's like asking a mother whether her baby is the third or fourth most beautiful in the nursery." Even as she wondered at her choice of analogy, she hurried on. "I feel a personal attachment to my pieces. I wouldn't sell any either, if I didn't need the money."

"My point exactly. Your personal sentiment supercedes the relative value of the article. These mountain people are the same—though they are not as much of a businesswoman as you are."

His innocent reference to the business side of art brought Gillian's mind to the appointment she'd have with John Regan at Dawson Textiles when they returned. As much as she wanted to share this prospect with her husband, she forced herself to wait until she could present him with a fait accompli, savoring in anticipation the pride she would feel.

"Why did you go into printmaking, Jill?" His dark gaze was searching.

She shrugged, taking a sip of her coffee before answering. "I seemed to have the inclination and the talent for it, I guess."

"But why printmaking, as opposed to working strictly with watercolor or oils?"

As her answer formulated, she couldn't hide a grin. "I guess I do take after your mountain folk—or your feeling about them. It really was very difficult for me to sell my work at first. So much of *me* goes into each work that, when I first started with canvases, I felt that something of me was lost as each sold. Printmaking has the advantage of producing multiple prints of the same image. Each set of prints is unique in that, once the stencil is destroyed, I can never exactly reproduce the set, but I do end up with sixty good prints, instead of one. I always keep several for myself. In a sense, I can have my cake and eat it too!"

"Smart girl!" he crowed between bites of danish.

And so it went, an easy camaraderie, as they traversed the area, each subtly learning more about the other as the days wore on. They visited the Qualla Reservation, home of the Cherokees, where they stood among the other visitors watching native women, replete with the traditional garb of full pleated skirts and bandanas pounding corn meal with mortar and pestle. They visited Grandfather Mountain to see the awesome replica of the old man in slumber. They passed the last of the old operating mills, its giant waterwheel turning to produce a buckwheat flour unique in texture and quality from those of the more modern electrically driven mills.

They paused to explore an abandoned schoolhouse, a rambling building from the first of the century, closed and deserted since the thirties. Rows of ancient Sears-made wood and iron desks, with folding seats and badly stained inkwells, faced the large potbellied stove at the front of the room.

"There were families and children aplenty in those days," Jed mused, his towering frame ambling slowly through the rows, almost anachronistic in the setting. "Then came the Great Depression. The land had been overfarmed, the forests decimated by overgreedy logging concerns. The children left with their families in search of greater bounty. How mistaken they were," he added softly.

Gillian had paralleled his path and now studied the yellowed portrait of George Washington hanging high on the wall. "You love these mountains, don't you?"

"The 'Great Blue Hills of God,' the Cherokees called them. I can understand why. They lift you higher than the mundane, above the everyday."

"Do you have any business interest here in the hills?"

"No." Irrevocably.

"Why not? You seem to love the people as much as the land."

He struggled to express himself, his hands thrust into the back pockets of his jeans, his head lowered. "Selfish reasons, I guess. My business interests are further toward the city. These hills are my home, my sanctuary."

She couldn't argue with his reverence—or his reasoning. As much as his corporation could potentially assist the economy of the mountains, there was always that chance of diluting the natural wealth that had, over the last half-century, finally regenerated itself.

As they retraced their steps to the schoolhouse door, she ran a wistful finger through the dust on a final desktop. "I would have liked the idea of my children being educated here." Absently, she placed a hand on her flat abdomen, only then recalling that possibility that a child was forthcoming. It was another puzzling reference. Instinctively, her blue eyes shot up to Jed's face to find him eyeing her cautiously.

Her whisper answered his unspoken question. "No, Jed, I don't know yet." In the split second before she'd spoken, there had been a hope in his eyes that she'd not expected. Did he *want* a child? Yes, in that instant, she would have sworn that being a father would have made him a very happy man. But, as always, the moment passed.

One evening, after a more quiet day around the cabin, he shanghaied her off to Linville and Wiseman's View, the best spot to observe the Brown Mountain lights.

"The Brown Mountain lights? What in the world are the Brown Mountain lights?" she had asked in response to the air of mystery he'd injected in his announcement of their destination.

"You'll see," was his only answer.

And she did. After an appropriately impatient period of anticipation, she saw it—a single small light skittering up above the horizon, glowing steadily there for several seconds before climbing higher in the air, hovering uncertainly, then winking out. They had watched through the windshield in utter silence, Gillian's eyes widened in disbelief, her breath held unconsciously. When strong fingers gave a mischievous pinch to the back of her neck, she cried out in fright.

"Jed! Don't do that! That is really eerie! What *is* that?" Her eyes clung doggedly to the horizon.

His voice was deep with intrigue. "According to legend, it is the soul of an Indian maiden searching for her brave, a warrior killed in battle."

"That's lovely"—she humored him—"but what *is* that?"

His broad white grin skewed gently in the evening darkness. "Don't believe the legend, huh?" She shook her head. "Well, neither do the scientists, but they can't seem to come up with a plausible explanation. They keep trying, but we mountain folk know . . ."

Gillian answered his singsong I-told-you-so with a good-humored "Humph!" then settled back to wait for another appearance of the mysteriously enchanting light.

The final excursion of the week was to Asheville, the Altamont of Thomas Wolfe's book. It was, as Amalia had suggested, uncannily as it was in the 1920s. Though reached now by a six-lane highway blasted through the mountain, rather than over the rickety red-earthed wagon path that Wolfe's Gant had traveled by coach, the streets were much as Wolfe had known them, Victorian houses stretching and winding for block after block. The country market was still in existence with farmers bringing truckloads of vegetables fresh from the fields and mountain women selling their colorful produce on long rows of wooden tables. It was an exquisite picture—sweet corn, fresh eggs, and country butter side by side with squashes, ripe red plums, lush purple eggplant, and jars of sourwood honey. The feeling was all here, Gillian mused with delight. It was as though the entire scene had been pickled and preserved, bottled for eternity in a transparent jar, packed safely amid the forest-cushioned mountains.

That afternoon, back in the Mercedes, when Jed's arm reached across the seat to draw her to him, Gillian slid willingly over, eagerly nestling against the warmth of his body. One firm hand remained draped over her shoulder as he drove; unknowingly, her own lifted to clasp it. A sense of contentment surged through her as the car coiled its way back through the rolling hills and hollows toward home, her own grip symbolic of her desire to cling to this heavenly serenity. Suddenly she wanted, more than anything, to be held fully in his arms, to be possessed by him, to be one with him again, as a fitting finale to this time of peace.

"I'm making dinner, tonight." If he'd read her thoughts, he mocked her, reminding her abruptly of his own promise not to rush her. What a turnaround it was, she rued, too well aware of the tingling inside for comfort.

Her voice was faintly breathy when she answered. "Didn't you like my coq au vin?"

"Your coq au vin was superb, as was your poached salmon, and your shepherd's pie. But it's my turn again."

"What is on the menu?" she asked, recovered from the moment's weakening.

"*That,* angel, is a secret. And *you* will have to stay out of my way while I work." It was a subtle reference to the first night they'd spent at the cabin, a night that seemed eons away.

But she obeyed his mandate without further argument, promptly disappearing into the meadow when they arrived back at the cabin. Actually, she welcomed the opportunity to bask in the joy of her love unobserved, undisturbed by lingering doubts as to the depth of Jed's own feelings. He'd been attentive and caring all week. In a stretch of the imagination, she might have thought him as much in love as she. But that was stretching it, as a harsh reminder of his reasons for marrying her proved.

Nonetheless, she was happy in this isolated mountain hideaway. In many ways, it had been that very isolation, that very change of pace from their life before, that had set these days apart. The haunting threads of the past were relegated to that other life; they had no place here.

As she wandered, kicking gently through high fields of broom sedge glittering orange in the late afternoon sun, she felt a surge of hope that the aura of happiness that had surrounded them here would follow them back to the chalet at Miller's Creek or wherever else their married lives would take them. Even without his pledge of undying love, she could live comfortably with this form of affection he did seem to feel. And if she were pregnant, there would be his child.

Her aimless stroll had taken her to the edge of the field, where the grass was near waist high, the wild flowers danced in the playful breeze, and the first of the evergreens began their ascent of the hillside. She felt light-headed and carefree, drinking in the fragrance of the forest as it tempted her, delighting in the soft swish of the grasses about her.

Suddenly, another sound came to her, and she froze. It was one she hadn't heard before, one she hadn't expected, one that came from directly before her. Instinctively, she knew its source. Terror paralyzed her limbs as her eyes searched the high strands. Then, heralded by a thunderous pounding of her heart, she saw it. Its head reared, wide and wedge-shaped. Its body, gently camouflaged by its black-brown pattern, was poised, prepared to lunge. Only its tail, the telltale rattle, moved, shattering the afternoon's serenity.

Revulsed by the thick body of the snake, its five-foot length coiled, she felt choked by the deadly menace of the head that watched her relentlessly, the tongue that flickered out at threatening intervals. Her mind was a blank of terror, her blood seeped like ice water through extremities that seemed suddenly far removed. It was a moment of panic, utter panic, a moment during which life passed before her, with lingering images of Jed and an unborn child holding a lure she might never taste.

It was a very different moment from those before the fateful plane crash. Then the situation had been beyond her control. Now it was not. She had walked innocently into the danger, imposing on the territory of this other creature, alerting him of her presence with the very vibrations of her footsteps. What should she do? Her mind had ceased to function.

It was an almost imperceptible change in the position of the hideous head that alerted her to the other presence. "Just move slowly, angel, back toward me. Very slowly. We don't want to frighten it." His voice was a bare whisper behind her, his firm hand slipping through hers a directional beam. "Come on, Jill, easy does it." His hand drew her back when her terrorized mind failed to register. Reflexively, her feet moved, though her eyes remained riveted on the rattler, subconsciously awaiting its strike. Gradually, as one timid step followed another, the wedged head receded. "That's it, angel. Keep moving. We're almost home free." Further and further he led her, turning her now so that she walked forward. When they finally left the tall grass behind and had entered the lower-cut meadow, he stopped. It was only when the strong band of his arms circled her that she yielded to a violent fit of trembling.

"You're safe now, angel. It's all over," he crooned softly, holding her to him as though to absorb some of her terror. Her arms went around him instinctively, her hands locking convulsively at his back. They stood in silence, each recovering from his respective trauma.

"I didn't expect it," she gasped tremulously.

"That was my fault. I should have warned you. The fear of snakes is built into these mountain people, but you had no way of knowing." His teeth clenched in self-reproach. "There are two kinds of poisonous snakes hereabouts— the copperhead and the timber rattler. It was that last that you met. He really is more interested in meadow voles and rabbits, thank God!" His arms squeezed a moan of agreement from her lips. "Are you all right?"

Her ear was to his chest, his heartbeat a steadying force. "How did you know it was there?"

A low chuckle erupted from deep in his throat. "You were like a statue. Pure stone. When you didn't move, I put the pieces together. Then I heard the rattle."

An involuntary shudder shook her, as she buried her face deeper against his chest. He was warm, vital. Her hands moved up the sinewed strength of his back. It felt so good, she mused, to be held like this, to be protected like this.

"Jill?" He'd sensed the change immediately. Had he correctly interpreted its cause?

"Hold me, Jed. Just hold me," she moaned softly. Having come so close to losing everything, she couldn't bear the thought of losing him now.

He echoed her moan with one of his own, as he enfolded her even more closely against him. The need to blot out the horrifying experience she'd just had was intense, as was the growing need within her, a need that had been nurtured by the intimacy of the week. This was to be their last night at the cabin. Gillian knew exactly how she wanted to spend it.

As she tilted her head back to look on his handsomeness, his fingers crept into the lush abundance of her chestnut mane. "Let's make love, Jed."

The gold-flecks glittered and deepened in their brown pools as he drew back to study her. "Are you sure, angel?"

She had never been as sure of anything before. "Please. I need you now," she whispered soulfully, reinforced by the tremor that passed through his body, flush against hers. Then he kissed her with the desire that matched hers, and she gave of herself completely. His lips lingered in firm possession as he swept her up into his arms and carried her to the house, passing easily through the kitchen and going directly to the room—her room, once his, now to be theirs.

Her legs slid down his as he released her knees, the friction between their bodies electric. He let her take the lead and set the pace, as slowly she unbuttoned his shirt and slid her fingers over the coarse mat of dark hair that furred his chest. Her lips followed, tasting him inch by inch, breathing in the tang of his sun-baked skin. So carried away had she become that she was temporarily startled when, reaching up to ease his shirt off his broad shoulders, she encountered his eyes. In a moment of unsureness, she hesitated.

His rasping voice urged her on. "Don't stop now, angel. You're apt to drive me insane. You're doin' just fine." There was none of the smugness she might have expected. Rather, his eyes held a tenderness that squirreled through her, tip to toe.

"You have such a beautiful body," she whispered as, in wonder, her eyes fell again to his shoulders and chest, rising and falling now with increased urgency.

"There's more, you know," he coaxed gently, taking each of her hands in his, kissing her palms in turn, then letting them drop to the buckle of his belt. When she struggled to release its catch, he helped her, leaving the zipper of his jeans to her questing fingers. He understood her need to explore, and, much as he craved to take her in the instant, he held his desire in check.

Gillian was oblivious of all but the glory of the male body that soon stood unencumbered before her. Her hands reveled in its firmness, her lips in its texture, her every sense in its raw sexuality. The level of his arousal thrilled her, giving her a taste of the power of her own sensuality.

Still, he gave her free rein, waiting until her need to lay her own flesh in contact with his was so great that she released him long enough to undress herself. There was an innocent seductiveness in her moves, inspired as they were by an emotion that transcended feminine wiliness, and that very innocence drove him to the limit of control.

A throaty groan marked the end of his passivity. "Come here, angel. God, how I need you." The sheets were cool against her back, a heady contrast to the heat of the bodies that met when he mounted her. Possession was quick and mutual, the pace of their passion spiraling to dizzying heights, before falling back amid a chorus of gasps and cries. When, after a bit, he filled her again, she knew a more leisurely rise to a height that even surpassed the first in mutual orgasmic ecstasy.

"You are a magnificent lover, Gillian Dawson," he crooned huskily, when finally he levered himself off and settled his long frame beside her. Within moments, they'd fallen asleep in each other's arms, satisfied and fulfilled.

CHAPTER 8

Then the honeymoon was over. As the Mercedes covered the miles between the Weaverville cabin and the chalet at Miller's Creek, Gillian anticipated the true meaning of that phrase. Those days they'd spent, just the two of them, had been wonderful, capped by the soulful lovemaking they'd shared on that last night. Now, however, the other life lay before them—one in which she would be forced once again to face the realities of existence.

"I'll be off for Durham in the morning," he had announced, when they had nearly reached their destination. It was the first of the realities she did not want to face.

"Must you go?" Her blue gaze darted hesitantly through the filter of long lashes. There was a dire need for her to cling to these days of togetherness that had meant so much to her.

His dark head angled briefly toward her before his eyes returned to the road. "Things will have piled up. I'll probably have to work doubly hard for several days. Yes, angel, I do have to go." He paused speculatively. "Will you miss me?"

Disappointment charged her point as she evaded a direct answer. "It's so lonely sometimes at the chalet." *Without you,* she added silently, afraid to voice the words that sounded positively cloying. In fact, she'd always enjoyed her solitude; this change in herself was a puzzlement.

Misinterpretation tensed the sinewed forearms that grasped the steering wheel. "Haven't you got things to keep you busy?" he asked coolly.

"Of course, I do, but—" An idea popped into mind,

lightening her expression instantly. "Could I go with you?"

"No."

"Why not?" All she wanted was to be near him. He was a source of strength, diverting her mind from more upsetting elements.

"I've got too much business to attend to."

"I wouldn't be in the way. I could even . . . wander around in the city on my own while you're working." The prospect was tempting, though she'd much rather explore the city with him by her side.

His tone chilled by several more degrees, confusing her further. "Do you miss 'civilization' "—he emphasized the word with disdain—"that much?"

Her denial was immediate. "No, it's not that. I just . . . I just wondered . . ." How could she explain without revealing the need she felt? And she was not quite ready to do that.

Immersed in thought, he continued to drive in silence. When he finally spoke, his voice carried the certain edge she feared. "Will you *fly* in with me?" The instant knot forming in her stomach told her that she was not quite ready to do that either. Her startled glance brought a thin grin to his face. "I didn't think so. Maybe another time, angel," he concluded, with a smug pat to her knee that infuriated her. The honeymoon certainly was over, she rued angrily, turning to glare out the window at the increasingly familiar landscape.

Jed left, alone, the following morning. Determined to make the most of her temporary, though enforced, widowhood, she quickly phoned John Regan to confirm their appointment for two days hence, then hit her studio with a vengeance, sorting out the preliminary sketches she'd made while at the cabin, mounting and shrink-wrapping the prints she'd finished before they'd left the week before,

170

then starting on a new series, the outline of which she was determined to bring with her to Greensboro. Her artist's eye conjured up a group of four prints, to be shown side by side on a continuous vista of bedsheet—if the project was approved—depicting a solitary yellow poplar, one she'd seen out beyond the pool, in each of the four seasons. Inspiration had actually come while driving through the roads around Weaverville, where the autumnal transformation had just begun. It was early yet; the dogwood and the blackgum had heralded the season with their deep red flourish, each new day bringing the next of the species—birch, buckeye, and beech—to fall coloring. Fully alerted, she would watch the tree she'd chosen, a beauty in shape and grace, as it approached, then reached its peak, before shedding its leaves for the winter's hibernation. It would make an exciting mural, she pondered as excitedly she set to work.

The director of the textile plant was as enthused about her concept as she was about her contract. She was introduced to a legal representative, a publicity representative, and several other plant personnel—all with the full intention of implementing the new line of silk-screened prints without delay. Throughout, she was careful to use her maiden name—a simple task, in that she could not yet think of herself as Gillian Dawson—thereby avoiding any potentially awkward questioning. She was eternally grateful that Jed had accurately described his role as minute in the everyday running of his plants; John Regan appeared to have full authority here, to make all decisions concerning the specifics of the products turned out under his eye. It seemed that the Southern Silk line, as it was to be called, was off to an auspicious start.

Exhausted but pleased, Gillian returned to Miller's Creek much later—later than she had planned—fully expecting to find an irate telephone message awaiting her. It was a mixed blessing to find none.

The tension began to mount the following afternoon as, attempting to transfer her sketch to the stretched silk and failing in the vital realm of concentration, she anticipated Jed's return that evening. Tired and cranky for a good part of the day, she had attributed her mood to the lateness of the hour when she'd finally fallen asleep the night before. Come midafternoon, however, she realized it was something else—the onset of sharp cramps assuring her that she was most definitely not pregnant.

Strangely disappointed, she tried to look at the positive aspects of this turn of events, but could find few. Even the knowledge that Jed's hold over her should be eased was no solace to the feeling of emptiness she felt. It was foolish, she told herself, to have expected to conceive so easily, yet Jed had presented his case positively and she, fool in love that she was, had chosen to believe him. She had begun to hope. Yes, hope. Though the thought of motherhood was a relatively new one to her, she realized she would have liked, very much, to experience that state.

Pale skinned and discouraged, she met Jed at the airport that evening, smiling in pleasure at his return, though taut with dread at having to give him the news.

"You look tired." He frowned, holding her at arm's length. "Are you feeling all right?" He didn't miss a trick, picking up on her pallor immediately.

"Sure. How was your trip? Did everything survive without you?" Mustering a teasing grin and a playful poke to ribs, she managed to redirect the conversation—but only for a while. Jed indulged her through dinner, until the two sat sipping brandy in the living room of the chalet. Only then did his manner grow more somber.

"Okay, Jill. What's wrong?"

Her head shot up in surprise from intent scrutiny of the wide rim of the snifter. "Nothing's wrong."

His eyes contradicted her. "Did something happen while I was gone?"

For a fleeting moment, but one of many similar ones since he'd returned, she was struck anew by the magnetism of her husband. Now, sitting at ease, legs stretched out before him, arms thrown casually over the back of the sofa, shirt unbuttoned to midchest, neck strong, face set, eyes compelling—she sucked in a breath involuntarily, then averted her eyes determinedly.

"I . . . I think I've found a market for my prints." The good news first, she reasoned, hopeful that he would consider it as such.

"You *think.*" There was an authority in his voice, something of an indignance that made her look twice. His had not been a question, but a statement. Not quite sure of her own reaction, she stared at him a moment longer.

"Ah, I *know.* But—so do you, don't you?" Defeat. She had wanted to do it all on her own and thought she had, until the message of his eyes had whipped that particular rug out from under her.

Slowly, he nodded. "Southern Silk. It's a fabulous idea." Silence hung heavily as he studied her downcast expression. "You don't seem particularly pleased."

"Oh, I am—about the project." Quickly, she clarified her feelings. "It's just that . . . I had really wanted to surprise you." Awkwardly, she fidgeted with the upholstered edge of her armchair, wondering where all her practiced poise had fled to.

"I *was* surprised."

"But you already knew!" Her blue eyes challenged him.

He leaned forward to rest his elbows on his knees. "John Regan approached me two weeks ago about an exciting idea that had been proposed to him by an artist. He had been looking for a new possibility; suddenly, he had it. Your timing was perfect. Your enthusiasm was catchy—he even chose the name of the line back then. I gave him my tentative okay on it before I was told the name of the artist who'd suggested the whole thing. Oh,

173

I was surprised, all right. I'm proud of you, Jill!" His fast-hardening tone took away whatever pleasure she may have felt from his praise. "What I don't understand"— steel underscored his words now—"is why you have waited this long to tell me." His anger was controlled, though that was little solace.

On the defensive, she explained. "I only found out about it for certain myself yesterday. You, it seems, knew about it before I did. When I last saw John, things were still pretty iffy."

His voice dropped. "You could have come to me beforehand, you know, to discuss the possibility—before you went to Regan."

She looked aside to escape his piercing stare. "There are certain things I like to do myself. I've always managed my career on my own. It meant a lot to me to do it this way. Call it pride, if you need to justify it further."

"And you didn't have enough faith in your own work to know that, whether or not you were related to me, you would have been able to get that contract?" His expression reflected his doubt. "That's an odd twist to pride."

Firmly, she took a final stance. "I just had to know for sure." She paused, reflecting sadly on what he'd told her. "But I don't know, do I?"

He leaned back decisively his voice begrudging in affirmation. "You know. It is a winning proposal. We would have gone for it had it been Jane Doe at our door."

Her faltering gaze lifted. "Then you do think it's a good idea?" His approval suddenly was all-important to her.

"Better than good. It's a fantastic opportunity for *you* and for Dawson Textiles."

A thought hit her. "You didn't let on to John that we were . . . married?"

His jaw had remained visibly tensed, belying his casual pose. "We weren't at the time I first discussed it with him. No, he doesn't know yet. But you'll have to tell him.

174

There's no other way to convince him to make the trips out here rather than having you drive the distance to Greensboro over and over again."

It was exactly the specialized type of treatment she didn't want. Protest was fast on her tongue and out. "But I want to visit the plant. That's half the idea. Most of my work is done in isolation; I need the contact with others for feedback. I enjoy seeing the workers there and would like to supervise the application of my designs."

A pulse of temper throbbed at his temple. "I won't have you doing all that driving, Jill."

"There's no harm—" Frustration burned in her eyes as she fought his domination.

"There *is*, Jill, if you're pregnant."

Now it was time for the bad news. Reflexively, she curled up into the chair and wrapped her arms about her middle, wishing she'd remembered to take aspirin earlier. "I'm not," she whispered, studying the shag carpeting.

The courage to face him slipped from her as, amid a prolonged stillness, she avoided his gaze. The rustle of movement caught her attention moments before his tall form lumbered to a crouch in front of her. The backs of his bronzed fingers feather-touched her cheeks; instinctively, her head tilted toward them.

"No wonder you're not feeling well. Is there anything I can do?" His concern touched her, even as his abrupt tenderness bewildered her. She'd expected a very different reaction somehow.

She shook her head, only then raising her eyes to his. "You're not angry?"

"Angry? How could I be angry, angel? It's certainly not your fault." The brown of his gaze melted into her.

"But that was one of the reasons you married me."

"One of them."

"I feel as though I've let you down." Once again she hung her head, her chestnut tresses falling forward on either side to her cheeks. He reached to comb them back with his hands, then took her chin with his forefinger.

"Are *you* let down?"

"I guess so. It might have been nice."

"There will be plenty of other chances, angel. You're still my wife, you know." His words curved in a smile, bringing a faint one of her own in echo.

"I guess so," she repeated wistfully, then took him on in mild accusation. "If you knew I'd been to Greensboro that day, why did you make such a thing about the mileage on the car?"

His brow furrowed. "I didn't know then where you'd gone. John didn't approach me until the beginning of the following week. I was away, remember? Afterward, I put two and two together, but I still don't like your doing such long driving alone." Deftly, he had brought the conversation full circle.

"I'll be all right."

His long frame straightened as he rose and walked toward the white brick fireplace. "How about a compromise," he suggested, slowly turning to face her. "We'll do it half and half. You can go to Greensboro when necessary, but Regan will come out here the rest of the time."

Once more Gillian felt manipulated, deprived of a freedom she'd long fought for. Standing, she stalked to the opposite side of the room. "You know, Jed, I feel like your prisoner again. Is that what this wedding band is all about?" Abruptly, she recalled what Amalia had once told her, and regretting her harsh words, she struggled to clarify them, turning toward him more softly. "I love it here, Jed. I have no desire to leave. But I'm used to having more liberty." His icy stare forced her on. "It's a very lovely feeling to spend the day in a new and, in this case, more hectic setting, then to be able to retreat here at night to the peace of the mountains. Isn't that what you feel? If you do it, why shouldn't I?"

176

Her plea had a ring of truth that Jed could not deny. Gradually, the gold flecks in his eyes warmed, sending their thawing message to her. The silent communication was as it had been so long ago in Essex. Several fluid strides brought him to where she stood, looking the distance up to his handsome face. His palms began a sensuous caress of her arms and shoulders, a strong finger moving to touch the faint starred scar at her throat. "I must be getting soft in my old age," he growled huskily.

Her lips curled into a soft smile. "You, soft? Never!" Her words were instantly muffled against his chest as she willingly allowed him to draw her into his arms. She had scored a victory. Perhaps there was hope for them yet!

"Don't get too smug, little lady," he drawled, reading her mind. "There's one advantage of keeping you in my employ, you know. I can keep closer tabs on you that way!" There was no way Gillian would have argued at his domineering direction, for there was, written subtly between the lines, a sentiment that thrilled her. It was a possessiveness that shunned pure domination, one that suggested a deeper emotion. But not wishing to dream further, she merely relaxed against him and enjoyed the moment.

As it turned out, her moment of victory was brief. To her chagrin, William was assigned the role of chauffeur, driving her back and forth to Greensboro for her once or twice weekly meetings with John Regan and the underlings at Dawson Textile. Not that she had any objection to William's company—he was a delightful guide through the highways and byways of North Carolina, giving her the continually narrated tour of the countryside and the city. Rather, her objection was an emotional one, sensing as she did that somehow Jed did not trust her. Even with Amalia's insights ever in mind, she had to work to stifle her annoyance. And there was that recurrent feeling—one that grew more unsettling as her professional life appeared to grow more settled—that there was still something she didn't know. It would come to her at night, when she'd awaken suddenly, reliving the scene of the airplane crash, on the verge of learning that which she couldn't seem to grasp—and Jed's steady arms would encircle her to still her quivering. It was as though, even in this gesture of comfort, he stole from her her gateway to the past. And though she never mentioned this haunting specter, she knew that she would never be fully at home, here, in Jed's beloved hills, even in his arms, until she finally discovered the truth. For the present, she accepted his solace, biding time until she was strong enough to take action on this dilemma. That time was to come sooner than she expected.

By mid-October, the forests were a vibrant mass of golds, oranges, and reds. To her delight, and subsequent dismay, the seasonal palette was as breathtaking as that she'd always savored in her native New England. And it was to the latter her thoughts flew as the days passed. It wasn't that she missed her old home for itself. After all, she had a new one, just as beautiful, with a husband who now filled a void she'd never realized had existed so subtly before. Yet there were old and unfinished matters in Massachusetts—her friends, the house she and Marika had shared, the artwork she'd left behind, and—and her parents' graves.

The foliage was at its peak of autumnal splendor when Jed bundled her up for a weekend at Weaverville. "You're in for a treat," he'd informed her, as she obediently packed her heavy sweaters to ward against the mid-fall chill. "They'll be making molasses at the Hitherroy farm on Saturday. We're invited to watch."

"Making molasses?" Gillian's own experience with the sticky brown stuff had been limited to one attempt at making Indian pudding, an abysmal failure.

His eyes glowed with a pleasure spreading to her. "It's an all-day affair, a social event in the mountains. You'll enjoy it."

She did. After a visit at Amalia's, they headed for the Hitherroy valley, irreverently forcing the silver Mercedes over the rocky road to a point where they parked, then continued on foot, side by side with other neighbors joining in the festivities. Jed greeted each with a warm nod or handshake, introducing his bride easily, seeming to be on a first-name basis with nearly all of the participants. As they entered the farm area, the red-streaked green stalks of sorghum cane greeted them, standing tall in the last moments of life.

It was a fascinating process, as Gillian was quick to discover. All hands chipping in, the stalks, with their fiery red seed spikes atop, were cut and stripped, then carted to mule-powered presses to be drained of their juice. Jed's arm lay slung about her shoulder as they watched the plodding animals, her own astonishment at the efficiency of the primitive method matching that she'd felt toward the old potter at work not far from here.

"I'm sure there must be more modern ways of pressing out the juice," she commented, "but none as charming."

"A mule, charming?" he ribbed her. Her answering elbow to his side was sufficient rejoinder. "It's not so much the end result with these people," he explained softly, "as the process. They look forward to this day as part of the fall ritual. It gives them a chance to see one another and to exchange news. In many ways it suits their purposes to drag the whole thing out for a day."

She smiled. "I envy them their leisurely pace. I'm a compulsive worker myself."

He lowered his mouth to her ear seductively, oblivious to the curious eyes that followed the every move of this handsomely matched pair. "That makes two of us." Then, he spoke louder. "Come on, let's get over to the furnace."

179

As they did, the eyes followed them, admiring the wife Jed had finally chosen, pleasuring in the peace that seemed to finally have come to their tall friend. Most of these mountain folk had known Jed from boyhood; most of them knew of Gillian's roots here. It was, in particular, the memories of the latter that caused many to intently study her features as she and her husband stood before the crude fieldstone-and-mud furnace in which large pans of the sweet, pale green liquid was starting to heat.

The fine, fragrant aroma wafted through the air, joining its complement of sensations for a permanent spot in Gillian's memory. There was the genial conversation, with its unique mountain twang, buzzing through the air in a low but steady hum. There was the casualness of dress—the workshirts and overalls, the full skirts and loose blouses, the sturdy boots all around. There were the children playing gaily in and around the operation, with the echo of frequent warnings to stay clear of the stone furnace. There were the smiles and the frowns, as word passed about a birth, a death, a marriage, a job, a layoff, or, surprise of surprises, the rising cost of gasoline. Jed and Gillian were warmly welcomed into the discussions, the lingering glances toward Gillian the only evidence of her recent arrival in their midst.

The latter bit of unsureness Gillian would very happily have overlooked, had it not been for one very pointed remark that was innocently made shortly after lunch had completely vanished from the long table set out for that purpose.

"A mighty pretty wife you got for yourself, Jed," one hearty whale of a man roared, slapping Jed firmly on the back before shaking hands with him in belated congratulations, then turning his imposing gray eyes to the subject of the discussion. "I remember your mam, Miz Dawson." His ruddy complexion grew even more so as the natural shyness of the semirecluse exerted itself.

"Gillian, please," she urged softly, grateful for Jed's confident hand at the back of her waist.

The great man grinned. "She was as pretty as you are, but you sure got the look of your daddy about you. Same eyes, clear as day."

"They can be pretty sharp, my friend," Jed warned humorously, his answer coming a little too fast. This time the feeling was acute, where in the past it had been more subtle. Gillian had *never* looked like her father—certainly not around the eyes. She was reminded of William's comment when she'd first arrived and of the interested looks cast her way even now by those who had known her mother. Here was one something she didn't understand. Unfortunately, there was not time to confront Jed on the matter, as he was called to take his turn by the furnace, stirring the bubbling mass and skimming off the layer of light green foam that was ever forming on its surface. It was a job he'd looked forward to since they'd arrived. With an indulgent squeeze of the hand, he was off.

Gillian mixed, timidly at first, then with greater confidence, with the others. She found them to be warm and open—not at all wary of her as they were frequently known to be of outsiders. Rather, they had seemed to take her into their midst and accepted her as one of them, despite their ogling. And that knowledge, gratifying as it was, gave her further food for thought. Casting Jed a casual wave, she slowly made her way to the edge of the group, where she found a solitary tree stump to sit on.

It was such a heartwarming sight, she mused, as she gazed back over the gathering. She did belong here. She knew it for a fact. This was in her heritage, something she, too, could look forward to year after year. Obviously, from the passing comments of many of those she'd met, her mother must have attended such gatherings. Had *she* felt as peaceful here? Had she felt the intangible lure of the hills? Had she ever missed them, once she'd left? Why *had* she left? Oh, yes, there was Gillian's father. But that was no explanation for her mother never having returned to visit. Surely Amalia knew more than she was saying. Surely Jed did also!

As though conjured up by thought, her husband weaved through the milling faces to reclaim her, an eager grin skewing across suddenly boyish features. "Here you are," he called, arriving triumphantly by her side, then allowing her to wipe the film of sweat from his forehead.

"Hot?" she asked innocently.

"You bet!" But he'd loved every minute of it. She hadn't seen him as exuberant. "I remember finally being allowed to stir that vat when I turned twelve. It was my rite of passage, so to speak."

"Oh?" The sheer earthiness of him was intoxicating, driving other thoughts aside. "Is that when you became a man?"

He caught his breath at her note of teasing, then grabbed her arm. "Come on," he urged softly, leading her toward the huge and aged barn that lurked, yards off, on the horizon. "That little comment will cost you." The huskiness of his tone heralded his intention.

"But, Jed, we can't—" she protested, half-running, half-walking to keep up with his lusty strides.

"Hush!"

"Where are you taking me?" As if she didn't know.

"To the barn."

"Jed, there are people—"

"Keep still, woman."

"What *are* you doing?" He'd reached and drawn her into the semidarkness of the barn and now searched its length, finally spotting the wide ladder. Even in the dim light, the gold sparks in his brown eyes danced in bright flame.

"Hang on." In the next instant she found herself being hoisted up over his shoulder, carried like a sack of

182

potatoes up the ladder, and finally deposited unceremoniously in the middle of the deep hay.

"Jed . . . ?" His gaze was unmistakably mischievous, his expression unmistakably hungry. Before she could protest, he threw himself down upon her, pinning her to the soft straw bed, his hands spread-eagling hers above her head, his legs intertwining with hers. *"What are you doing?"* she whispered loudly, not wholly displeased with the situation. They hadn't had a light moment like this since their honeymoon. No, even more, this was a whole new side of him—a carefree, irresponsible side that totally charmed her.

His voice was a hoarse rasp. "I've been wanting to do this for years. A romp in the hay with my girl." He paused to study her moistly parted lips. "You are my girl, aren't you?"

Subtle as was the inching of his body over hers, she reveled in the muscled strength of his arms and shoulders, the great firm width of his chest, the slim tapering of his waist and hips, the sinewed hardness of his thighs. His scent drugged her, his gaze drove her to distraction. Without so much as a kiss, he had ignited the hungry fire in her.

"What if someone comes, Jed?" Her whisper was as hoarse as his.

"Then they'll have quite a show, won't they?" The devil played in his eye as he studied her, making no move to release her hands, though his marauding gaze had her breasts straining against the fine fabric of her blouse. *"Are you my girl, Jill?"* he repeated in a single, more serious instant.

"You know I am!" Her reply was barely audible, yet it returned the wicked grin to his face, replete with dimple, both of which were subsequently lost to her view as his head lowered and his lips devoured hers, slanting in a frenzy that swept her to full arousal. "Oh, God, Jed, what

183

can we do?" she begged, driven mindless by the aching need for him.

He pulled back a moment longer, weighing their chances of privacy; then, looking around, he deftly rearranged the deep hay, enclosing them in a topless cocoon that only an ignorant peeping Tom would have dared to violate.

"Now be a good girl and get those damned jeans off," he growled huskily through a grin, his hands already moving to the snap of his own and working furiously. "We haven't got much time."

They didn't need much time, each as hungry, each as ready as the other. It was a memorable romp, explosive and fulfilling, binding them together for the rest of the afternoon as partners in crime. For when they finally returned to the molasses making, hand in hand and flushed with satisfaction, it was obvious to all that there had been some hanky-panky up yonder. Yet they were a delight to see, newly married and happy; no one would have dreamed to question their short absence.

Later, after the bubbling goo had thickened into full-fledged molasses, been poured into glass jars and bottles, then passed around, the mountain folk began their trek down the hillside, Jed and Gillian among them. The sun had burned to a bright orange crisp beyond the ridges, the chill of evening having soared in. Only when Jed's arm pulled her close to him, hip to hip as they walked in harmony, did she think again of how much she belonged here—and of how puzzled she felt because of it.

She waited until they were in the car and had left the last of the neighbors behind to ask him. "Jed, what do you know of my parents?" Had her hand not lingered in his, she might never have noticed the slight, but definite tensing of his fingers.

"Not much." Slowly, he measured his words. "I remember seeing them at several of your openings. I never got to know them."

"I mean before that—when my mother was younger . . ."

"Whoa, I'm not *that* much older than you!" She was getting too close for comfort. He took his hand and put it opposite the other on the wheel. As much as she regretted his withdrawal, a deeper need drove her on.

"I keep sensing something. It's the same thing I've felt since I woke up in the hospital. Even now, some nights when I suddenly wake up I sense it, too. There's something I should know, but I don't. I can see it in the eyes of all these people—but I can't see it myself. It would seem that I'm more blind than Amalia!" Her pale blues implored his help. "Do you know what it is, Jed?"

"I know that you have a vivid imagination."

"No, I didn't imagine the way these people look at me, as though they're seeing someone they knew a long time ago."

"They're curious, angel." He softened his tone coaxingly. "You're new here, and they're interested in you."

Stubbornness spoke through the firm set of her jaw. "No, I'm sure there's something else." Unconsciously, she raised her thumb to gnaw on its tip.

"Did you enjoy yourself today?" His voice was remarkably smooth once more, its depth announcing that that other subject had been dropped for the day. She let it go, pleased to have back the relaxed Jed she'd temporarily lost. Yet the thoughts lingered on in their regular nagging fashion. Things were so lovely. If only this mystery could be solved, she might feel free to finally declare openly her love for Jed, a love as far-reaching, she knew now, as that very mystery.

In her heart the confidence had grown that she could win Jed's love if she could finally give totally of herself. Yet to do that without being lost to his commanding personality, she needed the strength of full self-understanding. And for that she needed the solution to this mystery.

During their lighthearted lovemaking in the hay, she had realized that she could never again be whole without Jed. In that total emotional union was to be the fruition of her individuality. It was a vicious circle, with neither beginning nor end. And it was slowly, very slowly, strangling her from within.

CHAPTER 9

It was quite by accident that matters were brought to a head. Jed had left, as usual, on Tuesday morning to return to Durham, having spent the day before, also as usual, working in the office next to Gillian's studio. Gillian, in her studio, had just begun to apply another stencil to the surface of stretched silk, when Alicia called to her from the hallway.

"Phone call for you, Miss Gillian. It's Mr. Regan. You can take it in Mister Jed's room if you like."

Eager to hear what John had to say, she carefully rested her brush, put down the bottle of glue, and headed for the office, sending a quick "thank you" toward the form that already scuttled back toward the main part of the house. Since that first day when she'd explored on her own, she had never been into this room, other than in Jed's presence, and even then she had usually remained by the door, hesitant to disturb his work. Now, however, she crossed to the desk and lifted the receiver of the telephone extension.

"John? How are you?"

"We're doing great at this end, Gillian. How about you? How's the work coming?"

From the first, the two had gotten along well. She felt relaxed chatting with him. "It's exciting! I've just begun the summer stencil."

"Then I won't hold you for long. I just need some information. Measurements and all. Have you got a pencil? I'll tell you what I need, then you can call me at a more convenient time."

"Sure. Hold on." Quickly, she scanned the broad oak desktop for a pencil. Now that Jed worked here regularly, there were numerous piles of papers left for his return. With no sign, however, of a writing tool, she moved behind the desk to open the top drawer. Grabbing the first pen she found, plus a small pad of paper, she returned to the phone. "All set. Go ahead." As he spoke, her pen made the necessary notations. "Is that it?"

"For now. If there's more, I'll call again. When do you think you can get back to me?" His voice skimmed over the wire.

Her brows knit as she studied her notes, making mental calculations. "How about later this afternoon?"

"Perfect. Talk with you then."

Cradling the receiver, she looked over the pad once more, tore off the top sheet, and retraced her steps to the open drawer to return the pad and pen. She never would have seen it had the drawer not stuck as she tried to shut it. It was when she pulled it out again, further this time, that her eye caught on the thick packet that had been tidily stored in a far corner. At a glance, it contained letters—perhaps forty or more—secured with elastic bands both horizontally and vertically. They were thin blue envelopes, of the airmail type, with varied degrees of wear, some seemingly much older than the others. Reluctant to snoop, she would have reclosed the drawer—until she saw the handwriting. This was a script that she knew practically as well as her own. Heart in mouth, she looked to the upper left-hand corner, where the return address confirmed her suspicion. Then she looked lower, to find that the letters had been addressed to none other than her grandmother.

With trembling hands, she removed the packet. So her mother *had* kept in touch with Amalia all those years. Here were the letters to prove it. But what were they doing in Jed's desk? She made an instinctive move to return them once more, then halted abruptly. As much as she was the intruder, the lure was too great. Perhaps these letters held a clue.

Weak-kneed, she sank into the oversized leather desk chair. Then, driven by impulse, she removed the rubber bands and fanned the letters out before her. Their postmarks dated back to Gillian's childhood, the letters written roughly every six months. Timidly, she opened the most recent and began to read. It was a letter filled with news primarily of what Gillian's mother—even more so, Gillian herself—had been doing. The pride with which Sarah Montgomery had described her daughter's latest artistic accomplishments brought a lump to Gillian's throat. Quickly, she opened the next, then the next, in each case finding the same type of newsy correspondence.

Then, taking a deep breath, she reached for the bottommost letter of the pile—the earliest, chronologically, of all of them. Her hopes were high that, much as someone reading the last chapter of a novel first, she would find the answers she sought. But word after word, suggestion after suggestion, innuendo after innuendo brought her no closer to her goal of understanding.

"Tom is a wonderful husband," Sarah had written then, "and I'll always be grateful to him. He provided a solution to our problem that many another man might have shied from. I believe he loves me very much."

In a subsequent letter she wrote, "Please don't be angry, Ma. How can I go against my husband? He wants me to stay here with him, and I must. He deserves it, for what he's done." And, "My heart breaks for you. I was torn apart when I heard of Giles's death. He loved us all, as we loved him. I know what you must be suffering, and much as I would like to be with you now, Tom thinks it best I stay here. Try to understand him, Ma, just as I try to understand Daddy. They're alike in many ways. Stubbornness and pride can do such awful things."

Brushing the blur of tears from her eyes, Gillian read

from another letter. "The baby is beautiful! Tom is as happy and doting as I am. Fortunately, he never knew Alex or he'd see the resemblance immediately." Her stomach churned at the implication. *Alex?* Heart pounding in her stiffening form, Gillian sorted through the rest of the incidental news, searching desperately for sentences, even phrases, to clarify. In frustration, she moved on to the next letter, perusing it similarly. Here she read, "I want you so to see Gillian. She is your granddaughter. I have asked Tom to let me travel there with her, but he steadfastly refuses. I think he may be afraid that I won't return. His love is very possessive. I must be grateful." Then, later, "Has Daddy softened at all? I know how hurt he was by what I did; it was impulsive and irresponsible of me—can he ever forgive me? He would like Tom and he would love the baby. I have enclosed a picture of her. Will he at least look at it?"

Laying the letters down, Gillian buried her face in her hands, her fingers quickly growing wet. Her mother had suffered so much pain. But why? That she still couldn't discover. Determined to follow through what she'd begun, despite her own growing pain, she tucked her hair firmly behind her ears and off her fevered cheeks, then returned to the blue stack. But it was much the same. Hint after hint, but no conclusive statement. There was a distinct familiarity through it all, as though she'd heard it before, yet she was still unable to bring it back.

"I'm sorry that Daddy feels that way," Sarah had written later, "but I will continue to send you letters and pictures. If you choose not to show him, that must be your decision." The tone seemed to be noticeably hardening as the time progressed, chilling Gillian even as she read.

Several hours passed as she sat, mesmerized by these letters from the past, her past. Her stomach knotted in apprehension at the things she'd read, though she felt more confused than ever. It was when she had moved up through the years to the more recent letters once again that she began to find references to Jed. Each one disturbed her more.

"How could you have sent him, Ma?" Sarah had written in a fury, her scrawled handwriting reflecting the agitated state she must have been in. "Isn't it enough that I send news and pictures? Must he spy on us, too?" Then, in a later letter: "How could you do this? He's dangerous, just like Alex was. I don't like the way he looks at Gillian. He's typical of them—can't you see?" Then, once more, "He was talking with her at the opening yesterday. I know that she's been grown up and on her own for several years now, but he has a look of no good in his eye. I know that look, Mother!" Once more Gillian put down the letters. She remembered all too clearly the warning her father had given her, at the last opening, when she'd talked with Jed. Her father had suggested that men like Jed were a menace, seducing young girls heartlessly, and that she would be wise to avoid him. It all came back as though it had been yesterday. But there was so much more she didn't understand! The change in her mother over the years had been dramatic, as illustrated by the caustic thread permeating her letters. Only Sarah Montgomery's love for her husband and her daughter and her loyalty to her mother had remained intact.

Overwhelmed by this heartrending insight into the past, Gillian fumbled to gather the letters together. Only then did she notice the one that had fallen to the floor. It was thicker, heavier than the others. She cringed, sensing intuitively that it held something of even greater significance. Gingerly, she bent to pick it up, staring at it with trepidation for long moments. It had been mailed from Boston nearly eight years before. When an unknown force impelled her to raise the flap and withdraw the letter, a yellowed piece of paper, an old newspaper clipping, fell into her hand. It was an obituary notice for a man named

Alex Strimling, a lifelong resident of the mountains, it said—the last surviving member of the renowned Strimling logging family. *Alex.* Unsteadily, she unfolded the letter.

"Dear Mother," it read, using the more formal address that Sarah had taken to as time had passed, "Thank you for forwarding the death notice. It seems that Alex died very much alone, as well he should. Although it is wrong to speak ill of the dead, I cannot mourn his passing. He destroyed the family life we had and rejected one he might have had himself. For that I'll never forgive him. I do pity him, though, for he never got to know the daughter who would have been a source of great pride to him. She continues to thrive at college . . ."

The ink became a blue blur before her eyes, as she crumbled into the chair. The implication was clear—but could it have been? All these years Tom Montgomery had adored her. There had never been any hint that her parentage was not as it seemed. Yet could she refute these letters? It was something her mother would surely not have lied about! Why hadn't she been told?

The familiar nagging struck a chord in her mind, mingling with a newly throbbing headache. The letters had been sent to Amalia. Obviously, she was in on the deception. The letters had been found in Jed's possession. It followed that he, too, had known. Yet neither had seen fit to enlighten her!

Frustration erupted into a raw anger, aimed at her mother, her father, Amalia, and Jed. She felt hurt and let down. She was confused. It was as though the foundation of trust on which she'd thought her life had been built had buckled. There had been a gross delusion here, and she had been the dupe.

Dropping this last letter onto the others on the desk, she stumbled blindly through the house toward the room she and Jed had shared. There was a jumble in her mind out of which but one thing emerged—escape. She had to escape the emotional turmoil that engulfed her. Rational thought was impossible here, surrounded as she was by sights and sounds that could only remind her of the upheaval that had taken place in these hills twenty-eight years before.

Numbed by the discovery she'd made, she moved dazedly, opening her suitcase, packing it with underwear, slacks, blouses, skirts, and sweaters, then showering and putting on a soft-skirted suit that would be comfortable for traveling, throwing several toiletries into her bag, then closing it.

Neither William nor Alicia stopped her, if they'd even seen her, which her hazy state could not have known or cared. Backing the Mercedes out of the garage, she headed for the highway. Hours later, the train on which she'd booked a seat was heading north. Her destination, stop by stop, was not important. What *was* important was that she have a chance to breathe free of the oppressively haunting shades of the past that had possessed her for months now, since that plane crash in Vermont.

Her eye watched blindly as North Carolina faded into Virginia, then Washington, D.C., was left behind to yield to Philadelphia, New York, and New Haven. Late that next afternoon she arrived in Boston.

The excitement she should have felt upon this return to her native city, however, eluded her. Rather, she felt herself the wanderer, the aimless rover in search of a great unknown. Her mind was a blank as she walked the familiar streets, checking first into a hotel, then taxiing to the site of her parents' old house. Sold now and occupied by a new family—Jed had handled those arrangements with his usual efficiency, determined at the time to spare her further torment—the house looked just the same, as did the neighborhood, the city. It was she who had changed. Now she felt herself a mere visitor, a lonely one at that, just passing through en route to a more permanent home. Disconcerted, she returned to her hotel to spend a long and sleepless night.

Surprisingly, though, it was not the fateful letters and their implication that occupied her thoughts. On that topic she felt spent, burned out, suddenly weary, totally exhausted. No, she did not dwell on what she'd so inadvertently discovered in Jed's study. But gradually, as the numbness wore off and her senses showed signs of revival, her thoughts turned to Jed himself, to the inconsequential things, such as where he was, what he was doing, whether he had been able to find the car she'd left at the train station. It was an odd sensation, thinking of him when so many other seemingly more earth-shattering matters awaited consideration. Yet all she had to do was to look in the bathroom mirror to picture him shaving in it, or to look at the phone to hear his deep voice flowing over it, or to look at the unused pillow of the double bed to see his dark head resting on it. Try as she might, she couldn't shake his image.

Come morning, she took the train to Essex, again taking her time ambling through the streets, again feeling the visitor, the one whose heart was elsewhere. In an effort to combat the emptiness that assailed her, she took a cab from the center of town to the house that she and Marika had shared. The door was unlocked, as it always had been.

"Marika?" Her call echoed through the quiet house. "Marika?"

The response was distant. "Coming!" From the attic. Gillian was suddenly reassured by the normalcy of it all, bursting into a helpless smile when her friend plodded down the stairs, caught sight of her, and shrieked. "Jill! Thank God!" Bounding down the last of the steps, she quickly moved to hug her friend. "Are you all right?" Gillian nodded none too surely. "You look horrible! Did

194

you sleep last night? Where are you staying? How did you get out here? Jed was so worried!"

The barrage of questions floated by her—all but the last. "Jed?"

"Yes, Jed, dummy. Your husband? Remember?" Winding an affectionate elbow through Gillian's, Marika led her through to the kitchen. "Sit," she ordered. "You could use some tea, I think!" The kettle had been put on the stove to boil, when Marika returned to sit opposite her friend at the small butcher-block table. "Now. Answers."

Under her former roommate's prodding tongue, Gillian explained what she'd done since she'd left the chalet two days before. "It really is a boring story," she concluded, looking glumly at her lap. Even this return to the site of so much happiness for her had not eased the ache inside.

"I'm calling Jed. He'll want to know—" Marika began.

"No." At her friend's questioning gaze, Gillian continued, her soft voice pleading subtly. "Don't call him, Marika, please. I need time. I can't . . . face him just yet." Eyes downcast once more, the sting of tears touched her lids.

"Okay, hon. Let's have it. You've hinted at it on many another occasion on the phone. There's more to the story, isn't there?"

Driven by the need to unburden herself of all she'd learned, Gillian elaborated on the mystery of the past months—the looks, the comments, the eerie sense of the familiar—all leading up to the letters she'd read. When her narrative finally ended, the two sat in silence broken only by the whistling of the steam kettle. Tea was in cups in front of them before Marika spoke.

"What are you doing here, Jill? I mean," she interrupted herself quickly, "I'm thrilled to see you. But why did you come back?"

"I don't know. I just had to get away. I thought that

195

somehow things would be more clear here." She searched her friend's sympathetic face for comfort.

"But they're not, are they?" Marika smiled back sadly, knowingly.

"No." It was a meek whisper.

"You love him very much?"

"Yes." Even softer.

"Then why didn't you go to him with all this? He's the one who should be comforting you, not I!"

Gillian struggled to verbalize her thoughts for the first time. "Don't you see, Marika? I feel . . . manipulated. I feel . . . duped. He knew about all this, but he never told me. My grandmother knew, but she never told me. I can't believe that my own parents never told me. And there's still that big 'why'—why didn't my mother marry this Alex . . . if . . . if . . . ." Still she couldn't get herself to say the words. "I should know . . ." She shook her head in misery.

"Honey, that's all in the past. Jed married you in the present. Shouldn't that be enough? Shouldn't you be able just to pick up life where it is, here and now, and live?"

"But Jed sees me as part of that past! He married me mainly because of my grandmother." As she talked, a new thought struck her. "I've just learned that his father and my grandmother were partners at one point way back there. For all I know, he married me to get his hands on any holdings my grandmother may pass on. You know, he came up all those years to my shows simply because of my grandmother." She snorted and looked away in disgust. "And here I thought that I'd attracted him myself! No, Marika, he needed to get me back to the mountains. The accident helped his cause. And in the process he found a bedmate. He's never mentioned the word *love!*"

Marika was not at all taken in by her theory. "I could have sworn that I heard it in his concern, Jill. He was frantic—"

196

"He was angry," she interrupted loudly. "He was angry because I'd escaped him. He's worked so hard to keep me there—even to the point of marriage."

But her friend was staunch in her own conviction. "You're wrong, hon. And regardless, you owe him a simple call to say you're well."

Gillian considered the possibility, then shook her head sadly. "I can't."

There was a finality in her answer that Marika opted not to challenge. "Then what are your plans?"

In a moment of mental fatigue, Gillian threaded her fingers through the thick mane of her hair, closing her eyes tightly as though for an instant's rest, then sighing. "I guess I'll walk around a little more, visit the galleries, see our friends. At some point I'd like to go to the cemetery."

"Would it help if I went with you?"

Gillian shook her head. "No, thanks, Marika. I really need, more than anything, to be alone."

Respecting her wish, Marika offered her a tuna sandwich and the use of her car, then vanished back to her attic studio. Gillian took her up on both. But as she drove up and down the familiar streets, the emptiness returned with a vengeance, an emptiness that had nothing at all to do with her stomach.

Autumn's showing had ended here, only a few maroon leaves clinging stubbornly to the bare branches of the grand maples. The sight of even those few was enough to remind her of the recent weekend she and Jed had spent so gloriously at the cabin, their romp in the hay at the Hitherroy farm, their forays through the harvest-ripe countryside of North Carolina.

The town held its old charm, with galleries where, in the past, her prints had hung and triumphed. But her mind flickered back to the work she'd barely begun in Miller's Creek, the promising foursome, the roll of Southern Silk on Jed's velvet tongue.

The delight was spontaneous on the part of friends at seeing her. Each insisted on hearing about her work, her husband, her new home. But friends who had once been the very salt of her earth were suddenly merely a pinch. Jed—he was the salt of her earth now. If he were here, things would be complete.

Feeling forlorn despite an attempt at liveliness with Marika and several of the others over dinner, she returned to Boston, where the sheer weight of exhaustion put her to sleep. But there was no respite from her loneliness, she discovered, as she wandered through the city the next day, and the next. Things that in the past had always cheered her did no longer. It was ironic, she mused, that she should feel this void, when she'd finally unlayered so much of the mystery that had shadowed her relentlessly. Yet she walked with an air of near indifference, reacting to very little but the remembrance of Jed, lurking around every corner, at every turn.

Finally, after three days of solitary and futile soul-searching, she mustered the courage to visit the cemetery where her parents had been buried. Dressed in a warm wool pantsuit as precaution against the early November wind, she walked the well-kept slopes and paths for long moments before facing the inevitable. The shivering of her body was only indirectly related to the chill of the air; contrarily, it was more directly indicative of the emotional freeze that this spot inspired. The trees were skeletal, the grass a deathly olive. The cold stones stared sternly as she passed, begrudging the warmth of life at her command.

"Montgomery, Thomas Hastings and Sarah Cartwright," she read, "Beloved husband and father, beloved wife and mother." The dates were all correct, but unimportant. It was the 'beloved father' that held her eye. Yes, he had been her father—the only one she'd ever known. And he had been, he was beloved. Suddenly all anger seemed pointless. She had loved her father in life; now she loved him even more, knowing that he had taken another man's child into his life, into his heart.

Tears welled into shimmering blue pools as she drew her jacket together, then wrapped her arms about herself protectively. What did it all matter? Marika had been right. It was the past. There had been love, and that was all that was important. Her parents had given her everything they had. She'd known the best of each of them. How could she ever begrudge them their weaknesses? Lord only knew, she had enough of her own! Her thoughts flew to Jed, and she looked behind for him, half expecting, no, needing to find him close for support and reassurance. But all that met her gaze was the bleakness of the graveyard, instilling, in turn, its own form of bleakness in her.

On the distant rise, a group of people had begun to gather around an open grave, heads bent to rest on black-garbed chests, arms entwined for just that support she now craved herself. She shivered in empathy.

"Sad, isn't it, miss?" Startled by a voice behind her, she whirled around to find an approaching groundskeeper. "This is a sad business, to be sure," he went on, his hands thrust deep into the pockets of baggy green workpants, "but some are more pathetic. That one, there," he cocked his head toward the now fully formed group of mourners, oblivious to Gillian's dismay, "is a good example. Thirty-one years old, they say. On a vacation with his wife. Hit by a car on an unlighted road. A real pity."

Her eyes followed his to the rise, then dropped quickly to the ground as a spasm of terror seized her. My God, what if it had been Jed? What if he had been taken from me like that?

"Oh, excuse me, ma'am. You're a new mourner yourself, I see." His head angled toward the shiny-surfaced gravestone. "I'll leave you then." She barely heard him, barely knew he had wandered off in another direction.

For her thoughts were centered elsewhere. On Jed. Jed

had been right, way back there. Suddenly things grew crystal clear. He had been right; self-pity was an awful thing, and she'd been guilty of it repeatedly. How wrong she had been! She had so much, so very much to be thankful for. Her parents were gone, but she had their heritage. The old life was gone, but she had a new one. And it made not one whit of difference that it had been another man, one whom she had never known, whose blood ran in her veins. She was herself. She was an artist, a woman, a wife.

In the instant, she realized that, even if Jed had had ulterior motives for marrying her, it really didn't matter. She loved him. How much, she had only come to understand in these past few days of despairing loneliness. Everywhere she looked she saw him, for he had become a very part of her.

By nightfall she had reserved a place on the first train out in the morning, and that night, for the first time in days, she slept peacefully, finally understanding what it was she wanted. So much of it she already had; the only thing left to complete her purpose was Jed. If he didn't love her, she would settle for the genuine affection he'd shown on those occasions whose memory set her pulse to racing—in the hospital, when he'd made her laugh in spite of herself; at the chalet, when he had presented her with a studio built for her; at the cabin, when he'd retrieved her from the darting tongue of the rattler; then, later, when he'd consoled her on her disappointment of not being pregnant. There was something to hold on to there; she would simply have to cultivate it.

As the train clattered southward along the rails and the landscape reversed its patterned change, Gillian's gaze followed closely. The blue of her eyes was reflected in the window as she thought once more of the words of Thomas Wolfe. She was, indeed, very much alive in the meadows of sensation to which he'd referred, each one vivid, deep, and everlasting. Yet there was a larger, more far-reaching meadow, she now saw—one that encompassed the others, giving them an ultimate meaning. It was Jed, Jed's meadow, flaming with vibrant richness. All else was but a fraction; this was the whole.

It was this thought that lulled her, in harmony with the steady beat of the rail pulse, toward a sense of serenity. As Jed himself had said so many times, things would work out. They *had* to; she'd come too far to let them fail.

With the passage of the train across the final border into North Carolina, however, she realized that there remained an uphill battle to be fought. Despite all she'd learned about herself—her background, her desperate need for her husband—there was still the very same to be faced. Jed. She had run off without a word; she had deserted him. Now she was back, hoping to pick up where she'd left off. Was that possible? Would Jed be willing?

In anticipation, she had no inkling of what she might find. As each length of track brought her closer to him, however, her sense of guilt grew to immeasurable proportions. Her precipitous flight from him, much as it may have served her own purposes, had been totally selfish. Amalia had alerted her to Jed's fears; she had ignored them. Could she, in good faith, ask him to forgive her, to take her back into good graces that were slightly chancy to start with?

Too soon, the train pulled into Greensboro, and she descended to the platform, then made her way to a pay phone inside the station. The voice that answered the ring was impatient and hard, its curt "Yes?" confirming the worst of her fears.

"Jed?" It was a miracle that he heard her whisper.

"Where are you, Gillian?" The impatience underlining the use of her full name chilled her. He had been expecting her call, his anger gathering as he waited.

"In Greensboro. At the station."

"Don't move. I'll be there." It was a low order, barked imperiously, brooking no argument and punctuated by the slam of the receiver. As the line went dead, something within her followed suit. Unsteady legs carried her to a nearby chair, where she sank down in defeat. He had said it all in those few short words.

Time had no meaning as she sat, for an hour, even more, oblivious to the comings and goings of the everyday traffic, ignorant of the curious glances sent her way. She was a lonely figure, young and beautiful, though pale and unsure, the deep pain in her eyes blotting out all other sensation but the one that finally thundered through her consciousness.

"Let's go, Jill." The tone was as harsh as the steel fingers on her arm propelling her to the waiting car. When she dared glance up at him, his eyes held the road, denying her existence. She saw the tension in the hands that gripped the steering wheel, saw the controlled force of the profile, hard and unyielding. It was a short ride, filled with silent torment, ending at the gate of what she quickly, and to her instant fright, saw to be an airfield.

Courage was nonexistent; rather, it was fear that inspired her whisper. "Why are we here?"

"We've got to get to Black Mountain quickly. This is the only way." A jagged pulse throbbed at his temple, belying the impassive tone of his voice.

"Black Mountain? Why—"

"Amalia's ill. When you disappeared, she crumbled. Her blood pressure soared. She's been under sedation ever since." He did not spare a glance at her to sense her terror. "This is the least you can do for her."

Horror-struck, Gillian knew he was right. Not once had she stopped, in her selfish travels, to consider what her absence, so sudden and unexplained, would do to her grandmother. Her stomach knotted with such intensity, both at what she'd done and at what Jed was about to make her do now, that she thought she would be sick. A cold sweat betrayed her, yet Jed merely cast her a look of disgust, as, with a muffled curse, he swung his tall frame out of the car, stormed to her side, and gruffly escorted her to the waiting plane. His stride was long, impatient, and laced with fury. No word of encouragement was offered, as he coldly preceded her into the plane, hauled her in after him, then reached to fasten her seat belt. Panic-stricken, Gillian realized that this craft was a twin to the one her father had flown on that fateful day. The only difference was Jed in the pilot's seat.

Drained of all color, she inhaled deeply in an attempt to steady the jumping of her stomach and the shaking of her limbs. Her knuckles whitened as she clutched at the seat when the plane taxied onto the runway, gained speed, then took off, and when dizziness overcame her, she let her head fall forward into one of her hands.

"Try not to get sick all over the plane." The low growl was his way of telling her that he was fully aware of her discomfort. And she was too weak to react to his callousness, too weak to even toy with indignation or resentment. The pain within was too great—the memories, the fears, the knowledge that, whatever Jed's feelings for her had been, they were not strong enough to inspire either understanding or forgiveness. She had no way of knowing that his pain, just then, was as great as hers.

It was a nightmare relived in Gillian's mind, with flashbacks to that other flight and its final horror. This time was different, however, as they landed safely at the airport, then took a borrowed car to Amalia's. Conversation had been negligible, compounding her misery. Only when they entered Amalia's home did Jed pull her back to face him.

"Watch what you say, Gillian," he warned ominously. His eyes pierced her with dagger-sharp gold flecks. Involuntarily, she shuddered as she turned to climb the stairs.

The older woman's face was gray and weathered, more tired than Gillian had ever seen it. Timidly, she moved to the bedside and took a gnarled hand in hers. "Amalia? Amalia, it's me, Gillian."

After an interminable silence, the filmy lids lifted slowly and lifeless eyes met hers, puzzled, unsure. "Gillian?" The frailty of the sound was terrifying.

Forcing a tremulous smile, she whispered, "Yes, it's me, Grandma." Subconsciously, her grip on the limp hand tightened as, very gradually, a light returned to the old woman's sightless eyes.

"Oh, I've missed you so, child. We were so worried—" Her voice was weak, reflecting her words.

"Shhh, don't talk now. I'm here."

They sat in silence, grandmother and granddaughter, for a while, each deriving strength from the other. In the end it was Amalia whose delicate voice broke through the stillness.

"I thought you'd gone for good, child—just like your mother. I missed her, and I missed you. It was happening all over again—"

Sitting beside her on the bed, Gillian leaned forward to kiss the withered cheek. "It's all right now. I'm not leaving!"

"But where did you go, child? We didn't know . . ." A residual panic skittered over her face.

For the first time, Gillian's eyes left her grandmother's slight form to move hesitantly to that of her husband, whose rigid stance against the doorjamb had not altered since they'd arrived. Foreboding as he appeared, it was the frail woman on the bed who gave her the strength to speak.

"I had to go back . . . to Boston. There were things I needed to work out for myself there."

"And did you?" Deeply intoned, they were the first civil

words that Jed had spoken to her, yet the tall form that now approached the bed was menacing still.

She held his gaze for only a moment—"I think so"—before her blue eyes fell to her grandmother. "I had to visit the graves of my parents. It . . . took me a while to build up the courage, but it was something I needed to do."

The petite woman reached to trace her granddaughter's features cautiously. "Are you back to stay, child? Really?"

There was no hesitation in Gillian's response. "Yes, Grandma, I am." For she knew that she was, one way or the other. If Jed refused to have her, she would stay here with Amalia. But she was staying. The mountains were her home.

An airy smile spread over the pale features on the pillow. "That's good. It's all I need to know." She sighed, as much in relief as fatigue. "Now you run along and let me get my rest." As she patted Gillian's cheek, the younger leaned forward again to kiss her, this time lingering, savoring whatever strength her grandmother could bestow. It was the firm hand that took her arm from behind that brought her to her feet.

"Let's go, Jill. Amalia, we'll see you tomorrow." His grip remained firm as he ushered her back to the car. Once again, she was at his mercy, and, though the worst of his anger seemed to have passed, the warmth that Amalia's concern had instilled now dissipated quickly. She was chilled to the core by the time they pulled up to the landing strip and he jumped out.

"Oh, no, Jed. I can't go through this again—" Her head shook slowly as her eyes underscored her fear.

Once more his voice held no sympathy. "You'll have to. I've got to have the plane returned to the Beech Mountain strip by sundown. We haven't got much time."

A shaky hand grasped his arm. "Please, can't I stay here?"

"No." Insolently, his eyes fell to her hand, then raised

205

to spear her again. "Now get into the plane, Jill." His was a challenge, a dare that, had she any other option, she would have refused. But there was no choice.

Her agony was as severe as before, as Jed made the necessary preparations for takeoff. Even in the air, she suffered afresh from the old vision, the old tragedy. Sunset was coming quickly on, adding to the tension she felt in the tiny aircraft. Then the engine coughed.

"Oh, damn!" His tone was grave, much as another oath she recalled vividly. As in that case, she froze. As in that case, the pilot's fingers tightened convulsively on the yoke, his eyes fixed in dismay on the control panel. History repeated itself . . .

CHAPTER 10

"What is it, Jed?" Near panic raised the pitch of her voice by a notch.

Clenched teeth framed his growl. "I don't know." His gaze flew from one to the other of the gauges, while the engine continued its sputtering. Automatically, he reached for the fuel selector, switched it back and forth, then swore again. One hand reached to tap at the fuel gauge, a firm finger rapping at the needle, which hovered steadily at midpoint, then dropped abruptly to EMPTY.

"Fuel starvation. The gauge malfunctioned. Damn it, I should have double-checked." As in that other case, the pilot's trained eye scanned the expanse of hilly terrain below. Gillian knew only too well what he needed. Swallowing her terror, she joined in the search.

"There." He pointed to a straight, open stretch of meadow. "We'll go in there." Slowly, he chanced to gaze at her, his eyes finally soft and reminiscent of the man she had adored. "You know what to do, angel, don't you?"

Wordlessly, she nodded. Hadn't she been through it all before? In mindless movements, her fingers released the door locks, then checked her own seat belt and harness. Then, pushing her chestnut waves from her cheeks, she looked back at Jed. Never before had she seen a pallor beneath his tan; never before had she seen such tautness beneath his cheekbones, such grimness at his jaw. His eyes were glued to their flight path as the plane began its descent.

Fear throbbed violently through her veins. Last time there had at least been a wisp of disbelief; now she knew what could happen, what *had* happened once. With this moment of dread came a dire need to communicate, for perhaps the final time, with her husband.

Once more reading her thoughts, he spoke first, his deep tone resounding with cynicism. "Any confessions, Jill? Last words?"

"I love you." It was all she had to say. She said it only once, her voice an aching whisper, her pale blue gaze caressing his features with an intensity to last her through eternity.

Sharply, his dark head swiveled toward her, his own eyes searing her. "Damn it," he swore under his breath, his shadowed jaw clenching, his strong fingers strangling the yoke. But his reaction was above her comprehension. She only knew that she'd said her fill, that she'd spoken her heart. As her eyes mirrored her words, she felt relieved. For an instant.

"Hang on!" His teeth ground together. "We're almost down." It was a flashback to the past—the deathly silence, then the ungodly bump and clatter as the plane touched, then bounced along over the rough-hewn carpet of grass. Paralyzed with terror, she barely realized that the plane was slowing until, with one violent lurch, it came to a full stop. And then it all came back.

"Get out!" he yelled, his voice a roar in her ears. Blindly, she reached for the buckles of her seat belt.

"Get out, both of you!" he hollered again, a panic foreign to him now taking over. "Take her away, Sarah, and tell her. I'm trapped. I can't get out of this seat. You go! No, don't wait! It's going to blow."

"What can I do?" the woman's voice screamed. "Let me help you, Tom!"

"Go, Sarah! Gillian, push her out. You must! And tell her, Sarah! Tell her everything—and that I love her!"

The two women tripped, then fell from the plane and began to run, Gillian pulling her reluctant mother as the latter's cry rent the air. "Tom! . . . Tom!" Step followed step blindly, taking them away from the plane mere moments before it exploded in a deafening roll of heartbreak. Simultaneously, the hand in Gillian's grew heavily weighted. Amid the billowing black smoke and the noxious fumes, Gillian looked over her shoulder to see Sarah, hit by a piece of flying metal, writhing in pain on the ground. Horror compounded as she fell to her knees, struggling to remove her mother from the searing heat of the inferno in panic-driven tugs. Finally, away from the central cloud, she collapsed beside the limp form, oblivious to the excruciating pain in her own arm, only intent on cradling her mother's head, on willing her to live.

"Mom? Can you hear me, Mom? Please, don't leave me—Mom?"

A hidden resource, a sense of purpose, gave her mother the strength to grasp the hand that was held out to her. "Gillian, you have . . . to know. You'll live, so you have to . . . know." The voice was foreign, an alien gasp.

"Don't talk now, please . . ." Tears coursed down her cheeks as Gillian clung to her mother.

But Sarah sensed that there was little time left to do that which should have been done years before. "I was . . . with a man just . . . before I met your father . . ." She rushed on hoarsely. "A man . . . named . . . Alex Strimling. Our families . . . were archenemies. When . . . I became pregnant, he refused . . . to marry me. My . . . father disowned . . . me. It was your father, Tom . . . who gave us both . . . life. He loved . . . you, Gillian. Know . . . that." It was a strength born of sheer determination that drew out the words, though to Gillian's anguish it was fading before her eyes.

"I know, Mom! I know!" she cried helplessly, the words being irrelevant to the life–death struggle taking place.

Sarah's eyes glazed over, her lids flickered weakly, and it was a mere wisp of a gasp that subsequently met Gillian's ear. "Go to . . . your grandmother, baby. She wants

. . . you." She wheezed again, fighting for breath to the last. "He wanted . . . to tell . . . you, but he . . . was afraid . . . he wanted . . . for . . . so long . . ."

"Mom? . . . Mom? . . . No! . . . No! . . . No!" With each repeat of the scream, it grew louder, more frantic, until it had reached a bloodcurdling level. Then, against the ugly crackle of the burning wreckage, there was silence, darkness, oblivion, as Gillian passed out.

"It's okay, angel. It's okay. We're safe. Everything's going to be just fine." The croon was a heavenly music, coaxing her gently back from the far reaches of hell. "Just hold on, you'll be all right." With dubious consciousness came the feel of strong arms about her, a broad chest muffling her sobs, warm hands rubbing life back into her. Slowly, her eyes opened to the sight of the meadow at sundown, the last fiery rays of the sun blazing in innocent reflection on the bright metal of the plane, which sat, totally intact and apparently untouched, some yards from where she knelt, on the grass carpet, hugged tightly by Jed. Lest the peaceful image fade to that other horrifying one, she dared not move, but let the rapid heartbeat by her ear plead its case for reality.

The sensations were all there—the sinewed feel of him, the manly scent of him, the smooth hum of his voice. Then she looked up to see him, to know that he was real. The journey had been endless without him; now she devoured his every feature.

"I do love you, you know," she whispered in a breath broken by teary residue. She recalled his grimace, the controlled fury he'd shown when last she'd said it, but she didn't care. He had known so much about her that even she hadn't known; now it was time he knew it all.

This time, though, there was no anger in the fierceness that pulled her head back against him. "I know, angel." A wave of a shudder rippled through his muscles, echoing through to her in turn. "I've waited so long to hear you say that. A fine time you picked—"

Her head defied his embrace to stare at him once more, seeking an antidote for her bewilderment. "But you were angry   ?"

The softening of his eyes as they caressed her denied that emotion. "You bet I was. My wife finally tells me she loves me, and I'm about to bobble both of our lives. I've got the damned plane to land in a damned meadow, all because of my own carelessness. You boggle my mind, Jill, or I would never have taken off with a faulty fuel gauge!" Her pulse began to race once more, weaving doggedly through her confusion. "Do you have any idea how long I've been in love with you, angel?" Unable to fathom his words, she merely stared harder. "I first saw you at your college graduation. You didn't know that, did you?" Her astonishment was savored in a smug and satisfied grin. "Oh, yes, Amalia sent me that first time. But from then on, it was at my suggestion that those trips to Essex took place. Even after I'd been warned to keep a distance, it became harder and harder." He bent his head to touch his lips to each of her eyes. As he had willed, when they opened again there was a far different light in them; bewilderment had turned to hope. Tongue-tied, she merely listened, as he went on.

"It became an obsession with me." His hands molded warmly about her arms. "You were beautiful, intelligent, talented—and firmly ensconced in that artistic community of yours. It seemed a hopeless dream to get you down here with me."

Suddenly, he had gotten ahead of her. "My showings—why did you stop coming? I had begun to look forward to seeing you, I had begun to count on your being there, and then you . . . stopped."

"Did that upset you?" He clearly needed to know, and this knowledge pleased her.

Nodding shyly, she gave him the answer he wanted. "I wasn't quite sure why, but you added . . . something . . . to my shows. When I realized that I didn't have your address, didn't even *know* your last name, I was crushed."

Relaxation skewed his smile up handsomely. "Your mother kept Amalia informed of your goings on, and Amalia kept me informed. But"—he hesitated, thinking—"your father made it clear, once he realized who I was and where I was from, that he didn't want me around. I guess I was a kind of threat to him, though I couldn't understand why." Again he paused, studying the brightness of her eyes. But it all had to come out. Now was the time. "You saw the letters." It was a statement. When he'd found them strewn atop his desk, he'd known exactly what had disturbed her.

Guilt-ridden, she returned his gaze timidly. "I'm sorry, Jed. I had no intention of sifting through your desk. I had taken a call there from John Regan and needed paper and pencil, so I opened the drawer. When it stuck, I saw the letters—purely by accident."

She knew the cruelty of separation when he moved back from her and stood up. In one fluid move, however, he retrieved her hand and drew her to her feet and close again. "Let's walk, angel. I think my legs could use some stretching after that"—he cocked his dark head back toward the plane—"fiasco." As she fell into a shaky stride beside him, his arm circled her shoulder to pull her closer. "I didn't mind your going into my desk. I'm only ashamed that I didn't have the courage to show you the letters before you came upon them like that." A thought-filled silence separated his sentiments. "You know, the time you were away gave me a chance to think, too. I can finally understand your father, Jill. In many ways, I've done exactly what he did."

One of Gillian's arms was about his waist, the other raised to cover his hand with hers at her shoulder. Slowly, they wandered across the long-streaked meadow, heedless of the fast-encroaching dusk and their state of strandedness. The only thing that mattered was each other, and the truths that were at long last being aired.

"He was a good man, angel. You've known it all along, but I was too angry over what he'd done to Amalia, then what he'd done to you by keeping you in the dark for so long, to try to understand. He must have loved your mother very much to be so afraid of losing her back to the mountains. Just as I loved you so much that I was terrified to let you go, for fear you'd never return."

Gillian stopped, turned, then laced her tapered fingers through the dark hair at the nape of his neck. "I told you that I loved it here, and I do. But it isn't a case of black and white. It's what I tried to explain to you once. I can have both worlds—just as you do. It's not a question of one *or* the other."

His firm lips parted hers in a touch of tenderness, brief but eloquent. "I see that now, angel, but it wasn't always that way in my life," he murmured against her, then raised his head. "My mother and sister left. Went. No in between about it. It was mountain life versus city life. They chose the latter. I guess I assumed that in marriage there was that choice. After all, hadn't your mother left here, never to return? I was so stricken with fear that I couldn't hear what you were trying to tell me."

That he had searched his own soul was evident, and Gillian loved him even more for it. "But you have built a life that combines the two beautifully. Shouldn't that have told you something?"

A deep rumble of a laugh filtered through his well-formed lips. "Aah, but male chauvanist that I am, I did not conceive of any wife of mine doing the same."

Pale blue eyes challenged him skeptically. "You always knew I had a career . . ."

"And I was madly in love with you. Oh, I fought it. I

refused to admit it to myself. I didn't want to love any woman, knowing the potential torture I could open myself to. But when it came to you, I was helpless. When I finally accepted the inevitable, I planned my course of action. I thoroughly enjoyed building that studio for you." He swung her around so they could continue to walk. "In my own warped mind," he chided himself gently, "I assumed that I would be able to keep you locked between two rooms—your studio and our bedroom."

A coy smile broke out upon her face, revealing just a hint of white. "So that *was* why you married me."

"Partly." He squeezed her shoulder playfully, then grew more serious. "But mostly I married you because I couldn't live without you. You can't imagine the pure hell of sitting by your bedside at that hospital and wondering if you'd ever wake up. We barely knew each other then, yet *I knew.*" He chuckled in a rare moment of self-consciousness. "I would never have believed in that type of instant-attraction, love-at-first-sight type of thing—until you came along. You're in my blood, woman." He ended on a teasing note, but his words brought other thoughts to her.

"Tell me about Alex Strimling, Jed."

He paused to look at her, reading in her eyes the need to finally know. "He was ruthless, to be blunt. Good-looking as hell, but ruthless. From what I've been told, he seduced your mother almost by way of vindication for what had been an old, old family feud. There had been a lover's spat, a jilting somewhere, way back there. The two families never forgave each other. Alex was very bright, but a rogue."

For a long time she remained silent, absently studying the fall grass over which they ambled. "I could never understand my mother's rigidity when it came to my social life. She must have been terrified that I would be hurt the way she had been. But the magnitude of the fear she

214

taught me was unjustified." She spoke as though to herself. "It was so beautiful—right from the first." Then, remembering Jed, she looked up. "I only wish I'd understood her motives sooner. We all would have been spared so much pain."

Abruptly he stopped walking and drew her around to face him. "Don't blame your parents, angel. I know what your father must have gone through. He loved you dearly, yet he was afraid of losing that love. And the longer the deception continued, the harder it became to end it. *I* should know!"

Protest formed quickly. "I loved him, too. I would never have—"

"Shhh." He hauled her against him, into his embrace, and her arms clung helplessly to the sinewed strains of his back. "I know, I know. Love does strange things, though, whether it is the love of a father for his daughter or that of a husband for his wife." This time, when he kissed her, his lips spoke freely of his love. Finally released, she felt driven to answer that unspoken declaration.

"When I went to Boston, Jed, I was hurt and upset. I needed to get away. But as I walked around, there was this . . . this emptiness inside. I suddenly didn't want to be there, if you were here." Tears of emotion welled at her words. "I just wanted *you*." Sniffling, she swallowed hard. "Then I went to the cemetery, and finally had to accept the fact of my parents' deaths. It was too long in coming, but there had been so much turmoil inside since the accident, that I . . ." Her tremulous voice trailed off as she put a hand up to wipe the tears from her cheeks. "While I was there, I saw a funeral in progress. For a young man—an accident. And I thought of you . . . and if I'd ever lose you . . ." Soft weeping precluded further words. Reflexively, she buried her face against his throat and clung to his neck, her arms coiled in terror at the thought of ever letting go.

215

Silently, he held her until she'd begun to quiet, knowing, as on another occasion, of her need for release. She was so strong, as he'd told himself then, too strong for her own good. She had to learn to trust another to share her low times as well as her highs. But then, didn't he also?

Her voice was a warm murmur against his bronzed skin. "I was so worried you'd hate me for having run off."

"Angel, angel," he chided softly, "I could never hate you. Oh, I was hurt; at first, I was sure that my worst fears had come to pass, that you'd used those letters as an excuse to run off, away from these mountains. But then I grew more and more concerned about whether you were all right. I was close to panic when Marika finally called."

"She called?"

"Don't be angry. She's a loyal friend. She even told me to give you time—that she was sure you'd come back when you were ready. I was all set to run up there after you—"

All too clearly, she recalled the moment at the cemetery when she'd looked around for him. "Were you?"

"Damned right I was! And the waiting wasn't easy, I can tell you that! It was like sitting in the hospital all over again, wondering, not knowing. I did all my thinking and then I grew angry all over again that you'd run off without my being able to talk with you. Then Amalia got so sick—"

"I feel horrible about that! I should have thought to leave word, but I was so distraught at the time. Will she be all right?" Apprehension filled her eyes.

He grinned back, easing her tension instantly. "Oh, she'll be all right. She's one pretty tough lady. It's you I'm worried about."

"Me?"

As they walked on, engrossed in each other, the drying grass of the meadow yielded to the soft dirt of the evergreen forest. Now, in a brief glance over his shoulder, he eyed the grounded aircraft behind them. Turning his back on it again, he slid down to the ground against the broad trunk of a lofty pine, then pulled her down to rest against him. "I still have to get you out of this place. And I'm not sure you'll be terribly anxious to get into a rescue plane." Mischief danced in his eyes, to be reflected in hers with teasing accusation.

"That didn't seem to bother you earlier . . ."

"It bothered me!" he roared, suddenly vehement. "When it looked like you were going to either be sick or pass out, it bothered me. When it looked like your fingers were going to snap at the bone, it bothered me." No longer did his forcefulness intimidate her, understanding, as she now did, and appreciating, his sentiment. Struck suddenly by another thought, she interrupted him.

"Why did I think, all this time, that Allan piloted you around?"

"Would you have felt better knowing the truth?"

She blushed with a guilty chuckle. "No."

"I didn't think so. You never came close enough to see, and I didn't have the heart to disillusion you. I'm not that blind—"

"Oh, God, Jed, we've *both* been blind. Why didn't we see sooner? Why didn't you tell me you loved me?"

His breath fanned her thick waves, his sarcasm therein muted. "And give you that ultimate weapon to use against me? Now on the other hand," he alleged, "if *you* had confessed your love . . ."

"I was struggling frantically to preserve my own identity," she mused apologetically, "and I guess pride clouded the issue. Why couldn't we trust one another?" She lifted his tanned fingers to her lips, kissed them softly, then placed his hand against her cheek. So many, many times had she felt it there; now she could savor it unabashedly.

His voice carried a soulful depth to its croon. In her

217

heart she knew he meant his every word. "We will, angel, from now on."

Out of the blue, Gillian burst into gay laughter. Jed feigned offense, punishing her with a tightened hold of her middle. "Now what's so funny about that?"

She nestled her chestnut-cushioned head more comfortably against his shoulder, the better to breathe in his nearness as she savored his form of punishment. "It's not what you said. Your words were beautiful. It's just . . ."—she giggled again—". . . this . . . whole thing." In a wide gesture, she motioned toward the plane in the lower meadow, now bathed in deep purple hue. "It's us . . . here. We've just survived a nightmare, we are stranded, it's getting dark and cool . . . but I couldn't be happier." Her pale blue beams met his gold-flecked ones, and the two locked, as they always had, as they always would. Their communication was intense, vital, and soul-reaching. He understood her; they were of one mind.

"I love you, Jill. Nothing else matters." Tenderly, he kissed her, his lips caressing and worshiping first her own, then her face, feature by feature. "Unnh, come here," he growled as, in one adept movement, he had her on her back on the soft bed of pine needles, his own body falling sensually atop her. "What *am* I going to do with you? Rational thought doesn't even have a chance when you're around."

Thrilled that this effect, too, was shared, she beamed innocently up at him. "Now what would rational thought dictate here?"

Sturdy elbows held his weight as his fingers combed through her hair to immobilize her head, while his mouth devoured hers hungrily. When he finally answered, his breathing was ragged. "If I were of sound mind, I would go down to that plane to radio for help."

"The way I see it," she retorted playfully, "you don't need much help in what you're doing." His body had

218

begun to move over hers, the friction kindling a flame to heat them both.

"You're damned right, I don't," he groaned hoarsely, nuzzling her earlobe for a moment before hoisting himself up off her.

Memories of heated passion in a hayloft burned within her, unleashing a shock of disappointment that abated only when he grabbed her hand and pulled her up to join him. "I may not need help for what you have in mind, woman, but we will be stuck here all night if I don't get on the horn. I won't have you catching pneumonia. Don't worry," he added, amused by her crest-fallen expression, "it will take them a while to find us. And, in the meanwhile . . ." His smile skewed with triumph into a beauty of a dimple, the devil's unchallenged domain.

Then his lips seized hers again, tasting them eagerly, relishing her responding hunger. His bold fingers traced her shape from shoulder to hip, returning with maddening leisure over her stomach and rib cage, to arrive, finally, at the curved ripeness of her breasts. With devastating sureness, his thumbs found their tips through the layered thickness of her blouse and sweater, exacting from her a deep moan.

"How can you do this to me, Jed?" Her knees had quickly become a mass of jelly, her insides a fiery brew.

As he looked down at her, the gold flecks in his eyes flickered in eternal flame. "I've got every right, angel. I love you." On that indisputable note, they walked back through the blue-ridged meadow, arm in arm, hearts bound forever.

The unforgettable saga of a magnificent family

IN JOY AND IN SORROW

by JOAN JOSEPH

They were the wealthiest Jewish family in Portugal, masters of Europe's largest shipping empire. Forced to flee the scourge of the Inquisition that reduced their proud heritage to ashes, they crossed the ocean in a perilous voyage. Led by a courageous, beautiful woman, they would defy fate to seize a forbidden dream of love.

A Dell Book   **$3.50**   **(14367-5)**

The second volume in the spectacular Heiress series

The Cornish Heiress

by Roberta Gellis
bestselling author of
The English Heiress

Meg Devoran—by night the flame-haired smuggler, Red Meg.
Hunted and lusted after by many, she was loved by one man
alone...

Philip St. Eyre—his hunger for adventure led him on a
desperate mission into the heart of Napoleon's France.

From midnight trysts in secret smugglers' caves to wild
abandon in enemy lands, they pursued their entwined destinies
to the end—seizing ecstasy, unforgettable adventure—and
love.

A Dell Book   **$3.50**   **(11515-9)**